Copyright © 2023 M. Juan-Stanley all rights reserved

The characters and events portrayed in this book are fictitious. Any similarity to real persons, living or dead, is coincidental and not intended by the author.

No part of this book may be reproduced, or stored in a retrieval system, or transmitted in any form or by any means, electronic, mechanical, photocopying, recording, or otherwise, without express written permission of the author.

ISBN-13: 9798868413087

Cover design by: M. Juan-Stanley
Library of Congress Control Numb
Printed in the United States of

Acknowledgements

Thanks to everyone in the UK, USA and Malta who helped with this book, by editing, proofreading and suggesting improvements.

Very special thanks to Carol, Meg, Jana, and Stefan. Your help was much appreciated. And a final thanks to Microsoft spellcheck for almost always understanding which word I was struggling to type and only occasionally substituting an embarrassing alternative.

Chapter 1

The steamship, S.S. Duchess of Glen Coraige left the port of Heraklion and slowly followed the northern coast of Crete westward. Ahead of the steamship the sun was sinking to the horizon, over the calm blue Mediterranean Sea. It took several hours for the island to begin to fall behind the old steamship, but eventually Crete shrank towards the eastern horizon. Sitting on the rear section of the promenade deck, watching the ship's wake stretching out towards the distant island was Karolina McAllister.

Karolina was American, 'American by birth and Texan by the grace of God' as she liked to say. Twenty-three years old, she was the only daughter of a wealthy oil man and she was making her way solo across Europe, completing her own, individual and modern version of The Grand Tour. So far, she'd seen London, Paris, Florence, Rome and Athens and now she was leaving Crete bound for Malta in pursuit of her love of archaeology. She was proud, confident and independent. Her face had a natural beauty, with strong chin and cheek bones and a broad smile with full lips. Today she was wearing a light blue sun dress, with a cream-coloured sun hat. Her blonde silky hair was cut in a fashionable bob. Probably her most distinctive attribute was a pair of wide, clear, crystal blue eyes.

The sun was close to setting. Although it was pleasantly warming her face, it was also shining brightly into her eyes. Gradually the warmth and the peacefulness had seeped over her. Like her eyes, her book had become heavier, until she'd finally succumbed and dropped it into her lap. She felt that this was more of a time to meditate rather than read and she decided to just enjoy this peaceful moment instead.

Her mind began to wander of its own accord and she found herself thinking over the last three weeks on the island of Crete. They had certainly been exciting weeks, in many different ways. She had known in advance that she would love the time spent at the Temple of Knossos. Before she left America, she had been in communication with Arthur Evans who was in charge of the archaeological dig and she had received an invitation from him to assist in the excavation work. As a young woman with a passion for archaeology she had seen the three weeks working with Arthur Evans as the highlight of her Grand Tour. What she had not anticipated was that the excitement of the dig would be eclipsed by the murder of one of her fellow passengers on the steamship that brought her to Crete. Together with her fellow traveller, Alex Armstrong, they had been instrumental in bringing the murderer to justice. Meeting Alex was another of the unexpected events that had made the last three weeks especially interesting. At first, they had not hit it off and even now, as Karolina's mind drifted and she pictured him, she was still not sure what she thought about him. Twenty-five years old and undoubtably intelligent and quick thinking in an emergency, but most of the time Karolina thought of him as a schoolboy in a man's body. A very nice-looking body she admitted to herself. He was tall, just over six-foot and apart from an injured left leg, strong and healthy, with an attractive face and tussled light brown hair. She liked his hazel eyes, but always thought that they seemed to look sad or worried.

Karolina's eyelids had grown heavy and she was drifting off to sleep when she was awakened by a voice. It wasn't Alex's voice, as she had expected, but a fragile looking elderly lady.

"Would you mind if I sat here my dear?"

"No, of course not. You are most welcome."

"Thank you so much my dear. I won't stay long; I just want to enjoy a few minutes of sunshine before I go back to my cabin. Such a shame not to take advantage of such lovely weather and this beautiful view don't you think?"

"I do," replied Karolina with a smile.

"You have a lovely accent my dear. Is that from Australia, or perhaps South Africa?"

"America, actually," Karolina corrected her.

"Oh, I thought so. I'm very knowledgeable about such things you know. When one has travelled as much as I have, one knows such things. Although we have not travelled so much recently of course, what with the war and so on. It's become much less convenient. I'm Lady Felshaw by the way."

"Karolina McAllister. Pleased to meet you, Lady Felshaw."

"I saw you sitting here all by yourself and thought I wonder if the poor girl is lonely. Are you travelling with your parents my dear?"

"No Lady Felshaw, my parents are at home on their ranch in Texas."

"Oh, how wonderful. A ranch you say. I've heard so much about American ranches. Do you have cowboys working for you on your ranch?"

"Yes we do. Twenty-five of them. We have over a thousand head of cattle."

"So your father must be very wealthy my dear?"

"I suppose some people might say he is wealthy Lady Felshaw, but most of it comes from oil wells rather than the cattle."

"Really my dear? That's most interesting. Did he just find oil bubbling up on his ranch?"

Karolina laughed. "No. It was a lot more work than that. He was a toolpusher – that's the head of a crew of oil workers, but he read a lot and educated himself particularly on geology. Then he started wildcatting. Now companies come to him and ask if he'll prospect for oil for them."

"He sounds most entrepreneurial. But did you say 'wildcatting'? What on earth could that be?"

Karolina answered, "Wildcatting is risky. It's looking for oil, where none has been found before. It's partly science, partly skill based upon the look of the surface rocks, partly instinct and partly an awful lot of luck, or at least that's what my Pa says!"

Lady Felshaw had seemed to lose interest half-way through Karolina's answer to her question and now she started waving vigorously to someone out of sight behind Karolina.

"Horace! Over here Horace. Come over here at once Horace!"

Eventually the object of Lady Felshaw's attention came into view at Karolina's left shoulder and Horace introduced himself as Lady Felshaw's son. He was a rather delicate looking young man of about Karolina's age, five and a half feet tall with short dark hair slicked back against his head and a small fastidious moustache. His smile at being introduced to Karolina seemed to her to be a little sycophantic.

"Miss McAllister's father is a wealthy American oil magnate Horace!"

"Really?" said Horace, "So very nice to meet you my dear."

I'm not sure Pa would call himself an oil magnate, thought Karolina to herself, before she realised that Horace was continuing to talk, "Does your father have interests in Europe?"

By now Karolina was getting uncomfortable with the interest that Lady Felshaw and her son Horace were showing in her father's financial worth. Fortunately, a distraction arrived in the form of Alex. Walking slowly along the promenade deck with the help of his walking stick, he approached the group.

"Alex, please let me introduce you to Lady Felshaw and her son Horace." Alex acknowledged the introduction and lowered himself slowly and cautiously into the liner chair next to Karolina, before propping his walking stick against the arm and dropping his newspaper on the low table in front of them. Horace realised that the only other chair was some distance away from the small group. He went over to it and with some difficulty dragged it noisily to a position next to his mother's chair.

"Are you touring Europe, Karolina," asked Lady Felshaw, "Horace and I are doing a tour of some of the more fashionable and educational sights before we return to London and he settles down to raise a family."

"Are you engaged to some lucky young lady Horace?" said Karolina, a little surprised that any sensible young lady would be attracted to Horace. Then again, her mother would have said that there is always someone for everyone.

Lady Felshaw answered before Horace could, "No my dear, although many young girls have expressed an interest of course, but Horace has not allowed himself to be distracted by frivolous disruptions until he had established himself as a respected business man."

"And what is your business, Horace?" asked Alex.

Before his mother could butt in, Horace answered proudly "Sanitary ware. It's been our family business since my grandfather's day and when my father died, I took over the business. With Mommie's help of course," he said, smiling at his mother, who seemed less than pleased at Horace's description of their business.

"We are essential suppliers of quality products to the building industry" said Lady Felshaw, "In very high demand as our country rebuilds after the war!"

"Is there much rebuilding required in England?" asked Karolina genuinely surprised.

"Oh yes," said Horace, "There were dozens of Zepplin bombing raids and hundreds of people were killed and lots of property damage. Mommie and I hid in our wine cellar. It was so frightening!"

"Fortunately, our factory was undamaged by the bombs and is still in excellent condition, although as with any business there are opportunities for investment," said Lady Felshaw. "I'm sure your father would think the business a very attractive one that would secure the future for my son and his future family."

"And why would my father be interested in the security of your son's business?" said Karolina in low calm voice. Alex looked across quickly at her. He had cause to know that tone of voice. It usually meant he'd put his foot in it and was going to suffer. This time he felt reasonably sure it wasn't him, but that Lady Felshaw needed to tread carefully.

Meanwhile, Lady Felshaw, unaware of her peril, smiled back at Karolina, "Well, my dear girl, as I said, Horace has now established himself as a respectable business man and would be a fine husband for any sensible young girl. I'm sure your father would approve," and Lady Felshaw gave Karolina a smile that had more than a smidgeon of condescension.

"As wonderful a catch as Horace so obviously is," exclaimed Karolina, thinking as quickly as she could, "I'm sure my fiancé in America would not approve."

"Fiancé!" Lady Felshaw screeched. "The purser assured me that your fiancé had died in the war!"

Karolina by now was losing her patience with Lady Felshaw, who had obviously been checking passengers who might be eligible for Horace. "Well this is my second fiancé. You know how it is when one's father is an oil magnate. One is always on the look-out for eligible husbands."

Lady Felshaw looked at Karolina suspiciously. "And may I ask who the lucky gentleman is?"

Karolina's brain froze for a second. "Of course." Her eyes flicked to Alex looking for help. "He's very famous, but only in America of course. His name is . . . Hiram! Hiram B. . . Duesenberg! Hiram B Duesenberg," she said with a note of triumph in her voice.

Lady Felshaw looked at Karolina thoughtfully. "And what does Mr. Duesenberg do may I ask?"

"Well he's very wealthy of course." Her eyes flicked around looking for inspiration. "Railways," she said. "He owns his own railway actually. He's a millionaire of course. Owning his own railway."

"Really," said Lady Felshaw looking carefully at Karolina, and who is Mr. Armstrong who seems to be your constant companion?"

"Well, he's a detective," replied Karolina, thinking that at least that's a half truth. "Er, a Pinkerton Detective actually. A body guard, you know. So many kidnappings and ransom demands nowadays. Quite terrible isn't it."

Lady Felshaw looked disdainfully down at Alex. "I thought the Pinkerton Detective Agency was only in America?"

Alex met her gaze blankly. "Yes. Well, of course there is an overseas office in London," he said without changing his expression.

"Well, I think it's most irregular! An unmarried young girl travelling around with a, with a *tradesman* as a companion. I do not think this is how someone in your position should behave. This sets a very poor example. Come Horace, we will return to the lounge! NOW Horace!" So saying, Lady Felshaw rose and without looking to see if Horace followed, stalked off. After a few seconds, Horace rose and smiled awkwardly at Alex, then Karolina, then timidly followed after his mother.

"Outrageous!" exclaimed Karolina. "That woman was shopping for a wife for her son and had the nerve to think I would be interested!

"I think she was being perfectly rational, picking the most attractive girl on the ship," said Alex with a smile on his face, then realised that what he'd said was very forward and helplessly started to blush. "But very good quick thinking coming with your imaginary fiancé." Alex picked up his newspaper off the table and began to fan his face with it. "Interesting headline about the railways in England going on strike," he remarked. "And I see that the Duesenberg brothers did very well with their car in the Indianapolis 500 race. Relations of Hiram do you think?"

"Well she deserved it" she said. "She had the nerve to ask the purser if I was 'available'!"

She took a deep breath to calm down and sat there thoughtfully. Alex began to relax and started to believe that she had failed to notice his earlier unguarded compliment and resultant blushing until she said, "And that was a very sweet compliment Alex, even though there are many more beautiful girls on the ship."

After a pause of several seconds she continued, "Just in case you missed it, that was where you should have jumped in and told me that there aren't!" As Alex started stuttering his apologies, Karolina started to laugh. "Do stop it Alex, I'm teasing you! You can buy me dinner to make up for it when we reach Malta."

Chapter 2

The weather stayed fine the next day. After breakfast, Karolina made her way to the forward promenade deck and leant on the handrail. She was delighted to see a pod of seven or eight Mediterranean dolphins riding the bow wave of the steamship. She watched them for several minutes as they leapt and dived through the bow wave, keeping pace with the steamship with no apparent effort.

She was dressed in a long loose cream-coloured jacket over a cream blouse with matching joup-culottes. She had bought the culottes in Paris, thinking that they would be perfect for working on the dig at the Temple of Knossos. She now found they were also comfortable relaxed day wear. She carried her book, some sheets of notepaper and her fountain pen. She was determined to have a letter written and ready to be posted when they arrived in Malta at the port of Valletta. Also on her to-do list for this morning was Alex.

From his cousin on Crete, she had learnt that the injuries to his left leg had been sustained serving in the British Navy at the Battle of Jutland, early in the 1914-1918 war. As a result, he now needed the assistance of a walking stick. In the same battle he had also witnessed his father's death, when his father's battleship had blown up in one gigantic explosion and sunk, killing his father and most of the crew. Karolina had no way of knowing the deep trauma that continued to haunt Alex, or of the repeated nightmares he still suffered. She did know that after he had been injured, he had taken a desk job working for the British Admiralty in Italy and his work had been 'hush-hush'. That work was now over and he was on leave, prior to returning to England to be de-mobilized, or 'demobbed' as he called it. The only clue to the nature of his work that she had managed to discover so far was when he had inadvertently revealed himself to be a bit of a wizard with secret codes. As to his early life and family, she had found out very little except that he grew up on his family's farm on the Isle of Wight. One other thing she did know, from bitter experience, was not to offer him help because of his injured leg. His instinctive response seemed to be anger. He seemed to believe that it drew more attention to his injury. All-in-all, she was now beginning to realise that Alex, intentionally or not, had revealed very little about his earlier life. Several times she had deliberately tried to get him to talk about himself, his experiences in the war, or his injury, but somehow, he always manged to manoeuvre the conversation away onto other topics. She suddenly realised that he usually distracted her by asking her questions about her own life. One way or another he posed a bit of a mystery to Karolina and she was determined to solve it.

She had taken a seat and finished a three-page letter to her parents and was lying back with her eyes closed, enjoying the warmth of the sun on her skin when Alex arrived.

"Catching some beauty sleep?" he asked as he carefully lowered himself down in the chair next to her, and leant his walking stick against his chair.

Karolina slowly opened one eye and turned to look directly at Alex. In a low threatening voice, she said "Why? Do you think I need some?"

"What? No! No! You're already very . . . No of course I didn't mean that! Sorry!"

Karolina laughed. "Oh, Alex I'm sorry too, but you're so easy to tease; it's just too irresistible!"

Alex looked away feeling a little disgruntled. He felt it wasn't his fault that he kept putting his foot in it when he was talking to women. He had grown up in an all-male family and gone straight from boy's school to a boy's college, before enlisting in the British Navy at twenty. He had just had no exposure to females and especially none like Karolina.

Karolina looked across at Alex, who sat with his face turned towards the sea. She said seriously "I'm sorry Alex. Even though it's very difficult for me, I promise I will try to stop teasing you." She realised that even though he'd fought bravely in the war, in so many ways, he was still very much the young boy that he'd been before he enlisted. Mentally she shook her head. So many of the men who had survived the war had gone away to it as young boys and had no time to slowly grow into maturity as they should have.

Alex turned back to look at her solemn face. "It's okay," he said, giving her a boyish grin. "I'm just never sure when you're joking, or when I have really said something that annoyed you."

She sat there for a few moments longer, before deciding to raise a topic that had been puzzling her, since Alex had solved the secret code back in Crete. "Did you know that I've been trying to work out what your job was with the Admiralty? You'd said that you were just a paper pusher, but in Crete I found out that you had been doing something hush-hush. So then I decided that you were an international spy, who spent his time smuggling himself into enemy countries. Probably with a miniature spy camera, wearing dark glasses and a disguise!"

Alex laughed, "Don't forget the poison pill in my signet ring!"

Karolina was pleased. She wanted Alex relaxed for the next part of her plan. She avoided looking at Alex directly, but kept a careful watch on his expression out of the corner of her eye. As casually as she could she said, "Now I've changed my mind. I think with your maths background and knowledge of secret codes, you must work on decrypting enemy codes."

Karolina saw Alex suddenly tense up. After a few seconds pause, he replied in a deliberately expressionless tone of voice, "Sorry to disappoint but my job really isn't very glamourous at all. Just sort of pushing papers around. Just like I told you. A glorified clerk really," trying to make a joke out of it, he said, "I'm hoping it will help me get a job when I get back to England. Maybe I'll make a good accountant. What do you think?"

Karolina was sure she'd hit the nail on the head. He hadn't directly denied it, but had tried to redirect her. The way he had tensed up when he had heard her guess was good enough for her. Alex was a breaker of secret enemy codes!

She sat back smugly and smiled. She decided to let him change the subject. He had spoken to her several times about what he would do next, now that his work in Italy had come to an end, so she decided to ask, "Have you come to any decision on what you will do when you reach England?"

"I'm still thinking it through. I still don't know what to do." His term of service in the navy had ended, earlier than most, since those who had been wounded were demobbed first. At the end of the war, the

Admiralty had decided to shut down the office where he worked in Brindisi and made him an offer to reenlist and join a newly formed department in London. After more than a year of working practically round the clock and with little if any leave, he'd asked for and been granted some leave to rest and recuperate and also to consider the offer. He had decided to spend a few weeks with his uncle and cousin in Crete, which was when he'd met Karolina. After Crete, he planned to return to England via Malta and Gibraltar. When he got back to England, he would have to choose – either to take up the post the Admiralty had offered him, or to stay with his older brother in the small manor house on the Isle of Wight. If he was honest with himself, neither held much attraction for him. After his father had died, his older brother had taken over running the family manor house and farm and was making a good job of it. He knew his brother would welcome him back to the family home, but Alex really didn't see where he would fit in or how he would earn his keep. He didn't want to accept something that he worried would be very close to charity. His other choice was to stay in the navy. He felt that during the fighting, he had done important work, but he'd been mostly office bound and now that the war-to-end-all-wars was over, would the work be as satisfying? But most of all he just felt restless, wanting to be away from offices, to try something new, have new experiences, see new things.

Suddenly Alex realised that Karolina had been talking to him. "Sorry Karolina, I didn't hear that, what were you saying?"

"What I was saying," she replied peevishly, since he'd obviously not been listening, "was that my mother always used to say, if you're stuck trying to decide between two choices, neither of which you like, then create a third choice!"

"What would that third choice be?"

"Well, since I see the waiter approaching, maybe it would be a round of cocktails!"

Deciding that perhaps it was still a little early for cocktails, they both settled for glasses of fresh squeezed orange juice and coffee. Karolina spent some time explaining to the waiter how her coffee needed to be twice as strong as the coffee that had been served at breakfast. Still not sure that she had got her message across, she watched the waiter depart with their order.

Alex looked at the writing materials on the table next to her and guessed, "Writing to your parents?"

"Yes, I like to keep them updated on where I am on my travels. It made me really happy on our last day in Crete, when I received that letter from them. I hadn't heard from them in over a month and if their letter had been a day later getting to Crete, it would have missed me and I would maybe not hear from them for another month."

"You said your parents are both well?"

"Yes, Ma is all enthusiastic about the work the temperance society is doing in Texas and the Volstead campaign to prohibit the public sale of liquor. Pa didn't mention it at all, but I bet he's not so happy! He just told me all the news about our ranch and that he may be getting some more horses for the ranch. Oh, and he said Paraivo has sired a new foal and that he's sure it will win prizes!"

"Paraivo?" asked Alex

"Alex, I told you yesterday. Paraivo is my horse. It means 'chief' in the Comanche language."

"Sorry. Of course, I remember now. You were telling me about the fun you had riding your horse bareback, no saddle or stirrups. I was just a little distracted yesterday." What he decided not to say was that he had been distracted when she was telling him about her horse and her life growing up on their ranch, because her laughter and animation had made her face even more attractive than normal. That was something he would be much too embarrassed to ever admit to her. "Do your parents know you've changed your plans and are on your way to Malta?"

"Yes. I put that in my last letter from Crete. I wanted to ask you, have you been to Malta before and do you know if there is anywhere to buy more clothes in Malta?"

He laughed, "The Grand Harbour in Valletta is the headquarters of the British Mediterranean fleet, so I've been there several times, on board different warships, but I didn't really have much time to spend looking for dress shops, especially ones that sell modern fashionable clothes, like yours." Alex had been very surprised the first time he had seen her wearing her culottes, but now he had grown used to seeing her in trousers he thought they were quite attractive. "I have heard that Valletta has some very good markets and shopping streets though."

"That's wonderful. So, as well as owing me a dinner from yesterday, you can escort me round Valletta while I buy some more clothes."

Alex laid back in his chair, closed his eyes and let out a low groan. That was not something he had been hoping to do when they reached Valletta tomorrow. A day looking at women's shops was not high on his wish list. He took another deep breath and concentrated on enjoying the sunshine warming his face.

"You do know I heard that groan, don't you?" Karolina's soft voice interrupted his thoughts and prevented any further chance of him relaxing.

Chapter 3

The next day Karolina stood on the deck of the steamship as it entered Valletta's Grand Harbour, The day was sunny and hot and she was grateful for the slight breeze as the ship moved past the breakwaters into the protected harbour behind. The ship passed slowly between the forts of St. Elmo and Ricasoli with their sheer walls appearing to rise directly from the water. As the steamship sailed further into the Grand Harbour, the fortified town of Valletta on their right dominated their view. Valletta rose above the calm blue sea, built on the summit of a high, steeply sloping hill. A thin line of buildings squeezed themselves onto the quay that ran between the base of the fortified city walls and the water's edge. The walls that rose behind the quay were more than one hundred foot high. On the hill above the walls were visible the buildings of the city proper. Highest of all was the domed roof of the Co-cathedral of St. John. Across the harbour from this massive fortified town lay another fortification, Fort St. Angelo. Between them the harbour was busy with many naval and commercial ships. Largest and most impressive of all were the three battleships of the Royal Navy riding at anchor, in line, down the centre of the harbour. As well as a key strategic naval port, the Grand Harbour of Valletta was one of the key links in the Mediterranean commercial shipping network. Passenger ships and cargo ships also lay at anchor or were working their way out to sea. At the dockside she could see the quay was bustling with donkeys and carts, horses and carriages, with pedestrians weaving between them. Running along the quay were warehouses and colourful shop fronts, together with other buildings such as the magnificent gothic two-storey customs house. It stood on the quay with its large, central, arched entrance framed on either side by three ornate arched windows. As Karolina studied the fortified city, a mature, grey-haired single lady approached. She was dressed in a rather old-fashioned, full-length dark green skirt and matching jacket, with a wide brimmed hat, decorated with flowers. Even though the fashion was years out-of-date, she still appeared elegant. Two small, white dogs on lightweight leashes followed her obediently. As the elderly lady joined Karolina at the rail studying the city, she focused more closely on Karolina's choice of clothes. "I say my dear, are you actually wearing trousers?"

Karolina prepared herself to once more defend her modern taste in women's clothing, "Actually I believe the French call this particular style culottes. I find them very practical."

"I agree my dear and very attractive too. Good to see a young girl with both taste and a sensible head on her shoulders!"

"Why thank you!" said Karolina, taken aback by the unexpected praise.

"I wish that sort of thing had been acceptable when I was your age. It would have been ideal for climbing in the Alps"

"You've climbed in the Alps?"

"Many times, my dear! Back in 1864 I was one of the first women to climb the Eiger. I was one of the first to climb the Matterhorn as well! I might have managed a few more if I'd been able to wear clothes like you're wearing now," she said with a laugh.

"What did you have to wear instead?" asked Karolina

"Oh, most women climbers would wear full-length tweed skirts you know. We weren't supposed to be showing our ankles!" she laughed again. "It was all very silly looking back on it. I was lucky. I got Burberry to make me a skirt and jacket from gabardine. Much better than tweed or other materials and waterproof as well you know. I sewed some cords into the skirt at the hem and led them up to the waist. Put toggles around the waist as well, so I could hitch up the hem when I needed to."

"That's so ingenious!"

"Well, we had to be in those days. Couldn't just put up with having to do what the men thought we should, could we?"

"Absolutely not," agreed Karolina wholeheartedly.

"Even so, on a hot sunny day, the clothes seemed to weigh a ton," she lowered her voice and leant towards Karolina conspiratorially, "I remember one day in the Alps, I thought 'why should I have to put up with this!'. Took my skirt right off, hid it under a rock and continued climbing in the knickerbockers that I was wearing underneath!" She laughed again and stared at the view of the harbour for a few seconds, remembering. "You should have seen the guide's face. He didn't know what to do, just like a man. But in the end the joke was on me. When we came back down, I couldn't find the rock! Had to wait while the guide went back to my hotel room and brought me another dress. Damn fool brought me one of my evening dresses!"

Both she and Karolina laughed at her story and they chatted for a little while longer.

Eventually the steamship dropped anchor and immediately several small boats swarmed around offering their services as tenders to transport goods and passengers to the quay.

Making her apologies to Lily, Karolina left her at the rail and made her way down the stairwell to the deck below. Alex was standing by their luggage at the rail, where seamen were finishing securing the ship's stair over the side. Almost immediately one of the several tenders that were milling around the ship tied up at the bottom of the stairs. They were lucky enough to be offered places on this boat by the ship's officer in charge. Uniformed ship's porters soon transported their luggage down into the boat and they followed. Karolina smiled when she noticed Lady Felshaw and son hanging back at the top of the stairs so as not to have to share the same boat as her. Once all the places had been taken and a suitable fee agreed, the tender cast off. Its place as immediately taken by another tender and the process began again. Alex and Karolin's tender made its way purposefully across the harbour to the customs dock, vying for a place to tie up. Once moored, more uniformed porters were quickly at hand to help passengers onto dry land and to unload luggage. Alex and Karolina entered the customs shed, followed by two elderly, hunched porters with their luggage. Alex approached one table, while Karolina took the table next to him and the porters placed their cases on the tables for inspection. Alex's gave his passport to his customs officer and waited patiently as the officer flipped through the pages. When the customs officer got to the name page he stopped and looked at Alex's face carefully, before glancing to the side at a soldier standing by the wall. He was in the uniform of the British Military Police with the

Murder on Malta

distinctive red top to his peaked uniform cap. The custom's official gave the soldier a slight, almost imperceptible nod. It might have been a slight movement, but Alex caught it and looked up as the soldier, who Alex now saw was a sergeant, marched smartly up to him and saluted.

"Good afternoon, sir. Would you be Lieutenant Alexander Armstrong?"

"Since the customs officer just checked my passport, before signalling you, I don't suppose I can pretend otherwise, can I?"

Karolina, had also seen the approach of the soldier and was watching the conversation intently.

"No sir. I don't suppose you could," replied the sergeant. "Would you mind following me sir?"

Karolina immediately jumped into the conversation, "What's the matter? Where are you taking Alex? He's not going anywhere until you explain what's going on!"

"It's quite alright miss. There's nothing to worry yourself about. He won't be detained long."

"Detained! He won't be detained at all! I insist you explain what's going on!"

By now the sergeant was looking distinctly uncomfortable. Dealing with drunken sailors spoiling for a fight was no problem for him. Beautiful young ladies, elegantly dressed and speaking in an obviously well-educated accent, telling him what he must and must not do was a new experience. And he noticed that she was now stepping towards him quite assertively! He hurriedly took a step back. As he did so, another male voice spoke quietly from behind her. "There really is no problem, miss. Lieutenant Armstrong is not in any trouble." The voice was calm, deep and husky. Karolina turned around the see a muscular officer of about six-foot three with the insignia of a major on his Military Police uniform. He had blonde hair, blue eyes and was looking at her with a smooth self-confident smile that left her struggling for words. The major turned to the sergeant and he returned his salute. Still looking at the sergeant sternly he continued, "Sergeant Moore should have said he would be delayed for a few minutes, rather than he would be detained." Then he turned back to her again and the charming smile reappeared. "If it would reassure you, then of course it would be my pleasure if you would like to come with us?"

"Really, I have no problem with going with them," Alex said to Karolina. "We can meet up outside the customs hall?"

"No. I'm coming with you!" Karolina said, glancing at the major a little uncertainly. "That is if that's acceptable?" Why had she asked the major if it was acceptable! He'd already said it was. She'd just made a fool of herself, thinking Alex was being arrested and now she was asking the major his permission to go with him! She felt flustered and didn't know why. She realised that the major was smiling at her in amusement. She turned away and gratefully took her passport from the outstretched hand of the customs officer.

Casually the major ordered the porters to follow with the luggage and led them, Alex Karolina and Sergeant Moore through a door of the customs hall to a large adjacent anteroom. Once the porters had placed their cases on the floor and left, the major closed the door. Turning to Karolina, he made a slight bow, then saluted her and said "Major Fleming of the Military Police at your service and you are miss . . .?"

"Karolina McAllister, American citizen." Damn. Why had she added the bit about being an American citizen? It sounded so lame!

"Well Miss Karolina McAllister, American citizen, if you will permit, I need to have a quick confidential word with Lieutenant Armstrong, that will take just a few minutes and then I promise I will return him to you unharmed. Our thumbscrews and truncheons are all out being cleaned, so you need have nothing to fear."

Karolina knew he was quietly making fun of her, but he was so attractive and so charming that she really didn't mind and she realised she was smiling along with him.

Opening the door to the inner office, Major Fleming turned to Alex and said, "Lieutenant Armstrong, this way if you would please." He and Alex went into the office and shut the door behind them.

The office was small and utilitarian. There was one desk, with a padded brown leather office chair behind it and two simple wooden chairs without padding in front of the desk. The only other feature in the room was a small wooden table with kettle, teapot, half empty milk bottle, sugar bowl and several cracked mugs. Alex dropped himself onto one of the wooden chairs in front of the desk and propped his walking stick against it before remarking, "Looks like you take good care your prisoners."

Major Fleming laughed easily, "You're no more a prisoner than I am, as I think you well know!"

"I'm afraid I am a little at a loss," replied Alex. "Exactly how can I help you?"

The major looked puzzled for a second or two, then smiled. "Very good Lieutenant. I'm glad to see that you take security seriously until you establish who you are talking with. I should have identified myself correctly." He removed a folded ID card from his pocket and passed it to Alex. "Major James Fleming, British Military Foot Police and I have been read into the operation that brings you and your colleagues to Malta. I wanted to make contact as soon as possible and offer whatever assistance I could."

Alex studied the ID and then closed it and passed it back to the major. "Well, you're not British Military Police, I know that," said Alex, looking the major calmly, directly in the eyes.

"Really?" smiled the major. "And why do you say that?"

"Major is an army rank. When you saluted you used the navy salute. Hand held flat with the palm down. You should have saluted the army way, showing the palm of the hand to the front."

"You don't think my authority here in the customs house, recognised by the customs officials and with my sergeant-at-arms is proof enough of my identity, Lieutenant?" he said sternly.

Alex looked back at him and simply shrugged.

The major's face broke into a slow smile. "Excellent Lieutenant! Very observant of you. I will explain all later. You may not be sure who I am, but I know who you are. When your name appeared on the passenger manifest, we checked you out." The major opened the brown file he had been carrying. Alex could see his name and rank on the top sheet, with several paragraphs of tightly spaced typing filling the rest of the sheet. Major Fleming looked at the file for a second or two. "I know from your dossier, that you work for Room 40, the Admiralty codes and cyphers department and are currently assigned to the offshoot base in Brindisi, Italy. I'm also aware that it is being closed down now hostilities have ceased. I know this, because you and your colleagues have been temporarily

Murder on Malta

reassigned here to help me with a little decoding mission." Seeing Alex's confused expression, the major asked, "You did get notice of your posting to Malta?"

"No, major. I've been on extended leave and travelling for the last four weeks, prior to the end of my enlistment and returning to London to be demobilised."

"Ah! There lies the problem. A breakdown in communications! Even though we're the Mediterranean Fleet Headquarters, we don't know everything. People are always forgetting to tell us what's going on!" The major smiled and relaxed back into his chair. "Well, no need for me to push you to confirm or deny your role. Your colleagues will arrive from Brindisi later today and they can tell you all about what's going on. I'm sure we can sort all this out then. In the meantime, . . ." the major stood up and offered Alex his hand, "let me just welcome you to Malta and offer my help if you may require it during your stay."

Alex rose also and shaking his hand, followed the major back out into the anteroom to re-join Karolina and the sergeant, who were laughing together at some joke. Sergeant Moore hurriedly stood up and came to attention. Alex smiled at Karolina and nodded reassuringly to her. The major also smiled at her and then turning to Alex said, "It's rather busy in Valletta at the moment, but I have reserved a room for you at The Grand Harbour British Hotel. I'm afraid I didn't know your lady friend was travelling with . . .."

"I am NOT his lady friend!" Karolina exclaimed loudly.

"Er. . . no. Absolutely not." agreed Alex. "We're just, well, travelling together, that's all"

"Really?" said the major, smiling rakishly at Karolina. "That may be the best news I've heard all day!" Before Karolina could begin to object, he continued, "But I have some pull at the hotel and I'm sure the hotel will be delighted to find a room for such an attractive young lady. Sergeant, please arrange for a landau to take Lieutenant Armstrong and his . . . companion, together with their luggage, to The Grand Harbour British Hotel immediately." Turning to Alex and Karolina, he then said, "My apologies for the confusion," and looking at Karolina, "and any concern that caused you." before continuing to address both of them, "I have a table booked for dinner for you and your colleagues at the hotel this evening. Shall we say eight o'clock?" While Alex and Karolina both paused to consider their response to this offer, the major continued, "Good." Turning to Karolina he gave her a self-assured smile, "I'll be looking forward to your company!" Then turning on his heel, he was out the door to the anteroom and back in the customs hall.

Chapter 4

For several seconds Alex and Karolina stared at the door the major had just gone through.

Karolina turned to Alex and whispered, "You are going to tell me later what that was all about."

"I'm not really sure myself. It looks like there's been a breakdown in communications. Apparently, my colleagues from Brindisi are coming here on some sort of mission and the major assumed I had arrived to join them. I'll find out more tonight."

Karolina was brimming over with curiosity about what had gone on between Alex and the major, but was unable to satisfy it any further, because at that moment, the sergeant coughed politely to attract their attention. He said in a broad Yorkshire accent, "Excuse me sir, ma'am. If you'd be following me now, I'll be getting you and your bags to the hotel as smart as you like."

"Thank you, sergeant," replied Alex and, together they followed Sergeant Moore back into the customs hall. The sergeant barked out a command and pointed at two porters, who quickly collected the luggage. The sergeant turned smartly and marched quickly from the customs shed, with Karolina directly behind and Alex and the laden porters struggling to catch up.

Outside on the street several four-wheeled, four-seat, horse drawn carriages of distinctive 'landau' design were waiting for passengers. With a stentorian bellow of "You!!!" that made Karolina jump, Sergeant Moore pointed to the first of the carriages in line and then down to the roadway directly in front of him. The carriage driver cheerfully obliged by leisurely pulling his carriage forward and stopping in front of the group. He jumped down and assisted the porters, who had by now caught up, with loading the luggage. The two largest bags he strapped to the luggage rack on the back and threw the two smaller bags up onto the raised driver's seat at the front. Once the bags were secure, the driver jumped back up onto his seat and the sergeant took up position next to the step up into the carriage. With slight bow, he offered his arm to Karolina and said, "Ma'am."

Replying with, "Thank you sir," and smiling at him, Karolina placed her hand lightly on his arm and sprang gracefully up into the carriage.

The sergeant, after assisting Karolina, offered his arm to Alex. Alex shot a threatening look at him. Turning to the porters, Alex tipped each one with a few coins. Refusing any assistance from the sergeant, he grabbed either side of the carriage doorway with both hands. Placing his good leg on the step first, he heaved himself up into the carriage, before falling back awkwardly into the seat next to Karolina. The sergeant climbed up and seated himself facing Alex and Karolina with his back to the driver before instructing the driver to take them to the Grand Harbour British Hotel.

The carriage followed the road along the quay, with the sea on the left and a line of one- and two-storey buildings on the right. They passed a mixture of boat houses, store rooms, shops, warehouses and domestic dwellings, many with wrought iron balconies overlooking the harbour. From studying the harbour as the steamship had approached, Alex knew that behind and above these buildings a street ran in parallel to the sea front with yet more buildings and behind that were the sheer walls of Valletta fortress.

Murder on Malta

After a short distance, the carriage veered right, up a steeply sloping road. At the top of the slope they turned sharply right again. Still climbing, they passed through small squares with attractive houses, and into a lovely airy park and before taking a wide avenue back towards the fortified town. Eventually the carriage carried them to a large paved square dominated by the fortress wall on one side and by a massive baroque building in front of them. The building was heavily decorated with carvings and coats of arms. The sergeant saw Karolina looking at it and informed her "That building over there is the Auberge De Castille, miss."

"And what do they do there?" asked Karolina.

"That's our headquarters and where Major Fleming has 'is office." He smiled at her when she saw she was interested and continued to try to impress her with his knowledge, "and these 'ere carriages they call 'karozzin' ma'am."

"Thank you, sergeant. Sounds like you have been in Malta a long time?"

"Nearly a year ma'am."

"Do you like it?"

"S'wonderful ma'am. Fantastic weather, friendly locals. Better'n northern France I can tell yer."

The karozzin passed down one side of the building they had been talking about and then entered the narrow bustling streets of the town proper, so narrow, that there was barely space on either side of the carriage for it to squeeze through. Taking first a right then a left turning through the streets; they eventually came to a place where the street widened and opened out into a long plaza. As they entered the plaza, they could see the harbour laid out far below them on the right. The plaza sat atop the city walls. On its righthand side ran a thick three-foot stone wall, protecting traffic and pedestrians from the long drop to the roofs of the buildings below. Lined up against this wall were three karozzins, similar to their own, waiting for fares. On their left the plaza was lined by buildings rising seven or eight stories high. The faces of the buildings were crowded with blue and green enclosed wooden balconies looking out over the harbour. The last building in the row had a wide flight of steps leading up to its double doors, with a liveried doorman standing to one side. An elegant sign above the doors proclaimed it to be 'The Grand Harbour British Hotel'. Guests would have panoramic views from their rooms, over the streets and buildings below, and over them to the view of the Grand Harbour, and then across the waters to the fortifications of Senglea and Vittorosa.

Standing to one side of the hotel entrance were several horses, unharnessed from their carriages, drinking at a stone water trough. Their carriage drew up next to them and Sergeant Moore jumped out and marched up to the doorman in his uniform resplendent in gold braid and spoke quickly to him. Returning to the carriage, he again offered his arm to Karolina as she stepped down from the carriage, but respectfully moved away before Alex lowered himself carefully down. By now two young men, wearing less decorative uniforms than the doorman, had come out of the hotel and began to unload the luggage. The doorman held open one of the double doors leading in to the hotel and the little procession made its way in to the lobby.

Sergeant Moore approached a tall austere looking gentleman dressed in black tailcoat and grey stripped trousers and snapped to attention in front of him before announcing "Lieutenant Armstrong checking in. Major Fleming presents his compliments to you and requests one of your best suites for his other very important guest from the United States!"

The man turned and welcomed Alex and Karolina with an ingratiating smile. "Of course. Welcome. I am the hotel manager, Mr. Critchley. We would be most happy to accommodate the major's guests. Turning from them, he looked towards the receptionist behind the desk, a grizzled looking older man. The manager snapped his fingers to attract his attention. The older man didn't look up from the register that he was studying. Once more the manager snapped his fingers, again with no reaction. Then he called out "William". Still failing to get the older man's attention, the manager impatiently stalked over to him and bending down to bring his face to the same level shouted "William!"

William looked up at the manager. "Alright, alright. No need to shout!"

"You know very well you wouldn't hear anything less William!" snapped the hotel manager

"Ah well, maybe you have a point there," grinned the receptionist. Turning to Alex and Karolina he explained, "I got blown up by a mortar at Gallipoli. Docs fixed me up pretty well, but couldn't do much for my hearing."

Mr. Critchley failed to show any sympathy and told William, "We don't need to hear your medical history, William. A room for the Lieutenant and one of our best rooms for the young lady." Turning he gave Karolina another ingratiating smile, then left the group to greet an elderly couple entering the hotel.

"Now then, let's see what's the best rooms we've got available," said William. After a moment flipping through a thick book, he looked back up at Karolina and grinned. "Well as it 'appens, we do have a nice corner suite on the fourth floor and right next door we have a regular room for the lieutenant.

Karolina turned to the sergeant, "But the major didn't actually say anything about me getting a suite sergeant."

"No miss. Using me initiative I am. The major's always goin' on about usin' me initiative miss." In a quieter voice, he continued to her, "even if the major 'ears about it, he'll be fine with it. Bit of a one with the ladies is the major," and gave her a wink. Then in his normal voice, he addressed the whole group, "Right. Job done. I'll be getting myself back to the major. If there is 'owt you need sir, ma'am, then just be asking William 'ere to get hold of it. If he can't get it for ye, then ask him to get hold of me, Sergeant Moore. Pleasure to meet yer both!" and with a smart salute, he briskly marched out of the hotel.

William grinned at the two of them from behind the reception desk. "Just as the sergeant said, anything you need to make your stay happy, just ask for William and I'll do my best to arrange it. Now . . ." as he turned the register around for Karolina, "if you could just print your name and home address, then sign the register for me . . ." He offered her his fountain pen and as she wrote her name and address, purple lavender ink flowed smoothly from the thick fountain pen, to match the other entries on the page. When they had both finished, William turned the register back to check, then handed them two keys, with heavy brass key fobs. "If'n you'll just follow these two boys . . ." nodding towards the two porters, "they'll show you to your rooms."

Alex, Karolina and the two porters, made their way up the wide stairway from reception to their rooms. The first room they were shown to was Karolina's suite. They entered to find a beautiful sitting room containing a small elegant chest of drawers and in the centre of the room, two cream armchairs and an oak coffee table. In the corner was an oak writing desk, with an inclined, leather-covered writing surface occupying the middle third of the desktop. Either side of the desk's writing surface were small sets of drawers. Two archways led from the room one on the left and one to the front. These archways led out onto one of the enclosed balconies they had seen, but this balcony wrapped around the corner of the building from the front with views of the harbour, to the side, overlooking a small square set out with café tables. The archways to the wrap around balcony were hung with elegant cream curtains embroidered in gold. The room's wallpaper matched the curtains. A door on the right led from the sitting room to the bedroom which had another enclosed balcony, wardrobe, chest of drawers and a four-poster bed. Curtains, wallpaper and bedspread all matched the sitting room's cream and gold colour scheme. "Wow," said Karolina, "this is fantastic! Remind me to thank the major!" and she walked through the front archway into the enclosed balcony to admire the stunning views.

"Well, it was really the sergeant who requested it," mumbled Alex, feeling a little jealous of the handsome major.

"Whoever," said Karolina, over her shoulder, not really concentrating on Alex's comment. "Come and look at the view!"

Murder on Malta

Alex gave the two porters a tip and then joined Karolina in her balcony window. The view really was spectacular. Below in the harbour they could see steamships entering, leaving and moored in the port. A beautiful white steam yacht, with flags and bunting flying was anchored close to shore, almost opposite to the hotel. Below the plaza on which the hotel sat were two terraces of flat roofed buildings dropping down from the base of the city walls to the quay. The buildings were separated by a street running parallel to the quay and the wall. One building immediately below them had an especially long flat roof. Along the front edge, from one end to the other, stretched a line of blue and yellow flowerpots, planted with colourful arbutus and aloe vera. A young lady with long black hair in a ponytail and dressed in a colourful skirt and blouse was watering and rearranging the plant pots.

"This is so exiting Alex! Would you like to come with me and explore the town?"

"Absolutely. Give me a few minutes to settle in and I'll meet you downstairs in the lobby." Alex grabbed his small bag and his walking stick in the left hand and with his other bag in his right, he left her room and went to his own room. He noted regretfully that his room was much smaller and not so grand. At least it also had an enclosed balcony, even though it was also much smaller. A few minutes later he descended the stairs to the lobby area and not seeing Karolina, picked up one of the newspapers lying around and settled into a comfortable chair by the door to wait. As he waited and scanned through the newspaper, he kept glancing at the varied range of people arriving and leaving the lobby. Most of them could be quickly slotted into an obvious identity; businessman, tourist, military. A few were more difficult to pigeonhole: The tall African in full national costume who was being fussed over by a much smaller Chinese factotum. A scruffy grizzled old man, wearing the grubby oil-stained overall's that were the uniform of many ship's engineers, carried a small box wrapped in brown paper under his arm and was arguing with William on reception. Five European children of various ages, dressed identically, laughing and giggling were refusing to behave for their short, rotund nanny. The second oldest child was a pretty blonde haired little girl. She in particular seemed to be the bane of the nanny's life. She was constantly distracted by everything and everyone around her and in her desire to see everything that was going on.

Five or ten minutes or so later Karolina came bounding down the stairs into the lobby. She saw Alex seated in his chair and also noticed Lily Buchanan and her two small white dogs. Lily had apparently just finished checking into the hotel. Karolina approached her and greeted her.

"Hello again Lily!" greeted Karolina. "Everything OK?"

"Oh yes, my dear. I stay here quite often you know. The staff are very good to me," replied Lily with a smile.

"I'm just going out, but I hope we'll bump into each other again and perhaps have a cup of tea or coffee?"

"That would be wonderful," said Lily, "and enjoy exploring Valletta my dear." Turning, she followed the porter with her luggage, and led her two dogs out of the lobby.

Karolina crossed the room to where Alex was sitting. Alex folded his newspaper and clumsily began to extract himself from his chair.

He placed both hands on the arms of the chair and hauled himself upright, before reaching across to grab his walking stick.

"Made a new friend I see."

"Oh yes. Always making new friends." Karolina replied with a laugh. "Do you have any idea where we are going?"

"No. I suggest we ask William what there is around here." Approaching the reception desk together, Alex said to William, "We're just off to explore the town. Any suggestions?"

"Congestion, sir? No, it might be a bit busy, but no congestion."

Karolina leaned in closer to William. "No, William. Suggestions not congestion!" she shouted, laughing.

"Oh. Sorry miss. The gentleman needs to speak up a bit. So, suggestions you're wanting, is it?" William considered for a moment. "Well, you should definitely visit St. John's Co-Cathedral. It's very beautifully decorated and it's just a hundred yards away, directly behind the hotel," said William pointing behind him. "They have a very famous painting there, by Caral… Cavalgia… Cavaralgio … by a famous Italian painter. Not my cup of tea, but you two being educated will like it. Then there's the Grand Masters Palace. That's almost next door to the cathedral, that is. That was the palace for the Grand Master of Knights of Malta, ye' know, the Knights Hospitaller as they should be called. That's worth seein' as well."

"Sounds wonderful," said Karolina. "Thank you for your help."

"No problem, miss. Enjoy your day."

Chapter 5

Alex and Karolina walked through the double doors out onto the plaza. Going around the corner on their left they came to the café, with tables and chairs in the small square. Seeing some steps in a narrow lane ahead of them they began to climb further into the city. Soon after, the steps came out onto a busy street which they crossed and climbed yet more steps. The next street was wider and looked more important. Karolina asked one of the shop keepers which was the way to the cathedral and he directed them further down the street. Like their hotel, many of the buildings had either red, blue or green wooden enclosed balconies. Some were not only enclosed but had wooden fretwork privacy panels fitted to the windows. As they walked, they also studied the crowds of pedestrians thronging the shops and businesses along the street. They saw several women wearing the old, traditional għonnella. These were a form of head dress consisting of large circular hoods attached to short cloaks or shawls that were unique to Malta. Many were dark blue or black, but some were also decorated with white polka dots or white embroidered flowers. The men mostly wore European suits often with white straw boaters, or they wore the dark baggy trousers and loose shirts and flat caps of manual labourers.

It seemed like any type of item you might wish to acquire was for sale somewhere along this market street. Valletta's position on the trade routes was evident by the number of businesses involved in import and export, but also the wide choice of goods to buy. Lace, leather goods, jewellery, beer and wine, bread and other street foods, all seemed to be for sale somewhere along this street. Alex stopped at one of the food vendors and asked what the small pies were that she was selling.

"Pastizzi!" came the answer. Then seeing his puzzled expression, she said, "These you will like sir. Inside is very good goat cheese. These others are very good too sir. These have very nice peas inside."

Alex looked at Karolina and smiled enquiringly.

"Don't look at me!" she laughed "If you want to try one, go ahead."

"If I'm going to taste them then so are you!" he laughed. Turning back to the vendor he said, "Two of each please."

Alex exchanged a few coins for four of the small pies, then tentatively bit into one. "Mmm, this is good! Try one of the pea pies!"

Cautiously, Karolina took a small bite of the pie, before she too exclaimed in pleasure. "Crunchy outside but soft inside. It's not hot spicy but there are some spices there."

Meanwhile Alex had finished his first small pie and was starting on the second. "Mmm, I think the cheese ones are even better. Hurry up and try yours."

Happily, they finished their snacks and thanked the girl who had sold them, then continued on their way.

The Co-Cathedral of St. John was a few yards further on. A large square lay in front of the rather plain and unadorned façade of the cathedral. Either end of the façade was a bell tower reaching a few feet higher than the main building. As they made to enter, a hunched over old woman dressed in black from head to toe tugged at Karolina's arm and pulled her to the side of the doorway. From a small pile of black veils on a table she selected one and started to drape it over Karolina's head and shoulders.

"Oh, thank you so much. I should have realised," said Karolina taking the veil from the old lady. Fortunately, Karolina's arms and legs were already covered, but she adjusted the veil to cover her head and shoulders then put a few coins in the small pot on the old woman's table.

The old woman smiled and nodded enthusiastically before waving Karolina on into the cathedral.

As they walked from the entrance to the nave of the cathedral, they both slowed to a stop. As their eyes became accustomed to the dark interior, their gaze was drawn upwards. The high curved vaulted ceiling was completely covered by a stunning array of ornate and intricate religious paintings. Any surface that was not painted appeared to have been covered in gold leaf. As they stood there staring up at the incredible baroque decorations, a soft voice behind them broke the silence.

"It does tend to leave one speechless, doesn't it?"

They turned and saw a short, elderly priest standing behind them with a smile on his face.

"It certainly does," replied Karolina. "I think I've just truly understood the meaning of 'awestruck' for the first time."

"You may have seen how the roof of the nave is divided into six sections? Each section depicts different scenes from the life of St. John the Baptist."

"It's incredible. They look so realistic," said Alex

"I believe the painting may be even more realistic than you think," said the priest. "See the statues at the head of the columns? In fact, they aren't statues, but very clever paintings that appear to be three dimensional. May I ask, are you here today to worship, or for some other reason?"

"I'm afraid we're just ordinary tourists' father," replied Karolina. "We were told that the cathedral was so wonderful that we shouldn't miss a chance to see it while we're here."

"Please don't apologise. We are very proud of our cathedral and are happy that it gives pleasure to you."

"It certainly does. The paintings are truly incredible."

"The artist was Mattia Preti. If you are interested in art, you might also like to see our famous painting by Caravaggio, '*The Beheading of St. John The Baptist*' "

"I would love to see that father," said Karolina, at which he smiled and bowed his head before leading them further into the cathedral. As they walked, he showed them the richly decorated side chapels, one for each of the eight 'langues' or nationalities that formed the Knights of St. John. Finally, they arrived in the oratory. As before, they stood speechless in admiration in front of a massive painting dominating one wall of the oratory. The image of the executioner standing over the body of St. John The Baptist, watched by a handful of onlookers was both graphicly violent but also powerful and tremendously moving. Alex and Karolina stood silently for several minutes as the priest explained the symbology hidden within it.

Noting that Alex had been leaning heavily on his stick and shifting his weight awkwardly, the priest asked "Would you like me to bring you a chair my son?"

"No father. I'm fine" replied Alex brusquely.

Karolina looked at him quickly, realising that he had been on his feet a long time, and they had climbed several long flights of steps in their exploration of Valletta. "Actually father, I think we need to be going. I have to thank you for giving so us much of your time, but I regret that I'm beginning to feel quite tired now. Perhaps we can return another time to see more of your wonderful cathedral." The priest looked at her thoughtfully then glanced again at Alex. Nodding to her in understanding, he turned and led them back to the entrance door. Here he shook hands with both of them and expressed his hope to see them again soon. They emerged into the dazzling daylight and began to retrace their steps, back to the hotel.

As they finally reached the bottom of the last flight of steps, Alex was glad to see their hotel come into view around the corner. The prolonged walk and climbing of so many steps had been not only tiring, but painful for his injured leg. Not that he would ever admit to it. As they entered the lobby, Alex was very grateful to be in the cooler air. "I'm going to sit here for a minute or two to finish something I was reading in the paper. Why don't you go up to your room and I'll see you later for dinner this evening?"

"Agreed" said Karolina cheerfully, understanding that Alex was worn out and maybe in pain, and was looking for an excuse to rest before tackling the hotel stairs. She left him to his reading and took the stairs from the lobby to her room. Once she was out of sight, Alex immediately collapsed into the chair by the door and took out his packet of cigarettes, tapped one out of the packet and lit it. Inhaling deeply, he picked up the newspaper from the side table and started to glance through the headlines. Two short, rather portly, elderly female guests entered and smiled at Alex, before going into the lounge. By the time he had finished his cigarette and scanned through the newspaper, he decided he had recuperated enough to attempt the stairs to his own room.

Chapter 6

Dinner had been arranged for 8pm. Karolina came down to the lobby, dressed in the one and only evening dress that she had with her. It was dark blue silk, with a dropped waist highlighted by a broad contrasting light blue sash. It had a square neckline that artfully drew attention to her double string of pearls. It was a modern fashionable design that ended just below the knee. The fabric and the design made the best of her slim figure. Arriving in reception, she was immediately spotted by William, who called out to her. "Evenin' Miss McAllister. Major Fleming has reserved a private dining room for his soiree this evening. Lieutenant Armstrong's colleagues have all arrived, checked into their rooms and are already seated for dinner."

Karolina felt a little embarrassed to be the last to arrive for dinner, but decided to not let it worry her. She was looking forward to dinner with the attractive major and also with Alex's colleagues. She was hoping to learn more about Alex and his mysterious 'hush-hush' job from them. William came out from behind reception to lead her through to the private room. It was panelled in dark oak, decorated with oil paintings and lit by several wall lights. Sure enough, already seated at the highly polished, long walnut-veneered dining table were **seven people**. At the head of the table sat Major Fleming, smiling at her confidently, with two young ladies seated either side of him. The young lady on his left had curly blonde hair and was wearing a cream satin evening gown. Her lipstick was scarlet red, a little too bright and a little too heavy to be fashionable and she was wearing five strings of pearls which in Karolina's opinion was too many. Major Fleming introduced her as Violet Osborne. Seated next to Violet and rising from his seat to be introduced to Karolina was Violet's husband, Percy, with slicked back dark hair and a pinched unhappy face. Not enjoying the dinner by the look of him, Karolina thought. The final guest on that side of the table was introduced as Ronald Findlay. He rose to his feet and taking Karolina's hand kissed it, before saying "Welcome dear lady. So very nice of you to grace our little dinner party."

On the other side of the table, sitting next to the major was a rather plain young lady, with curly dark hair, who was introduced as Maude Cooper and who smiled a little shyly at Karolina, before nodding her head and looking down to study her place setting. Next to her sat a young man, smiling happily to himself, who rose from his chair. His gaze deliberately slid over Karolina from head to toe before he finally reached out to shake her hand. This, and he way he held onto her hand for a little too long, had her quietly fuming inside. Before the major could do so, he introduced himself as Robert Smith, "Delighted to meet you, my dear!"

Alex had been seated in the final chair on that side and smiled welcomingly at her before re-taking his seat as she sat down at the foot of the table across from the major.

"Well, well, well, Alex, I can see why you kept Miss McAllister a secret from us. She's quite a beauty!" said Robert.

Alex was clearly irritated by his remark and said, "I've not been keeping her a secret. We only met a few weeks ago on the steamship taking us to Crete."

Robert simply sat back, continuing to apprais smug smile on his face.

Major Fleming said, "Miss McAllister is more than just a pretty face. I hear from the authorities in Crete, that she and Alex were instrumental in solving a murder while they were there.

"Alex dear boy! You were supposed to be taking a well-earned rest, not chasing murderers around. You really must take better care of yourself," remarked Ronald with concern on his face. Karolina had a chance to study Ronald more closely as he berated Alex. He looked to be about fifty, very well groomed and like the other men at the table wearing dinner jackets and bow ties. In addition, he wore a rather fancily embroidered waistcoat. A cigarette dangled loosely from one hand and he sipped sherry from a glass in his other hand.

Alex looked embarrassed and said dismissively, "It really wasn't as exciting as it sounds."

"Nevertheless dear boy, you mustn't exert yourself. You must try to rest here, before we get the steamer back to Britain."

Karolina knew that Alex hated being treated like an invalid and for his benefit decided to change the subject. She turned to Maude Cooper and asked her, "Do I understand that you are also one of Alex's colleagues, Miss Cooper? Were you also based in Brindisi with Alex?"

Maude looked a little embarrassed at being drawn into the conversation but smiled nervously at Karolina and replied, "Oh yes. Brindisi was lovely. I'm very sad we're all going home."

Robert added smugly, "Maude is our little mathematical genius." Turning to the major he said, "If you need the bill for the dinner adding up, major, she's the girl to oblige you," and laughed at his own joke.

Maude blushed bright red and hung her head over the table so that her dark curly hair fell forward and hid her face. Karolina decided she did not like Mr. Robert Smith. "And your role Mr. Smith? Are you also a mathematician?"

"Oh no," answered Percy on his behalf. "Mr. Smith tinkers with wires and valves and things," sneered Percy.

Annoyance crossed Robert's face. "Damn lot of good you'd be without my work with the radios," he snapped back.

"Now, now, please boys," said Ronald. "Let's not spoil Major Fleming's kind invitation to dinner by falling out again. We're all part of a team and we should do our best to get along in these last few days together. Let's settle down and just be nice to each other."

Conveniently at this point, he was interrupted be the arrival of the first course, a vegetable soup.

"So, Ronald," said Karolina, "Is your job to keep the peace between the warring factions in the team?"

"Oh, they really aren't such bad boys you know," said Ronald placing his right hand over Karolina's for a second or two. "But someone has to point the troops in the right direction and shout 'forward!'."

"So, you're the boss?" Out of the corner of her eye she saw Alex struggling to hold back a smile.

"Oh yes, I like that! I'm the boss! Makes me sound very strong and manly," said Ronald.

Karolina noticed that Percy's habitual frown had turned into a badly disguised sneer at Ronald's comments. "I imagine keeping Alex under control would be a permanent chore," she laughed.

Murder on Malta

"Oh no darling, Alex is the sweetest boy. Never any trouble from Alex." Then, leaning in closer he whispered conspiratorially, "not like Robert and Percy."

Karolina looked across at the two men he'd mentioned and noticed that Percy's antipathy to Robert was not shared by his wife. She was smiling at Robert and looking at him from underneath her fluttering eyelashes. He was returning her glance with a rakish smile. Karolina decided she had a very good idea of what was causing the friction between Robert and Percy, and its name was Violet.

As the courses came and went, the atmosphere around the table didn't improve noticeably. If anything, as both Percy and Robert consumed more wine, it deteriorated. Percy became sullen and angry. Robert became boastful and obnoxious. He monopolised the conversation, talking about himself and how he had already ordered a new sports car that would be waiting for him on his return. He talked at length about what were the 'nicer' areas in London and his plans to buy a house in one on his return to England. Karolina found it more pleasant to converse with Alex and Ronald. Poor shy Maude seemed to have little to say to anyone, although a couple of times, Karolina did catch her looking at Robert, seated next to her, with a strange intense look. Violet continued to cast loving glances across the table at Robert. Her husband caught at least one of these glances and hissed angrily at his wife, who for a time afterwards, guiltily confined her attention to her meal.

As the dinner progressed, Major Fleming charmed each of the guests in turn. As they were approaching the end of their main course, Karolina found herself being drawn into conversation with him.

"It sounds like travel is one of your passions Karolina?"

"Yes, you could definitely say that, but I think my biggest passion is archaeology. For the past few weeks in Crete, I've been helping with the dig at the Temple of Knossos."

"You know there are some magnificent ruins both very near here and also on the island of Gozo?"

"Absolutely. Hagar Qim is south of here, but what I'm really interested in is the Temple of Ggantija on Gozo. Allegedly the oldest buildings in the world. When Alex said he was changing ships on Malta, it seemed like a great excuse to travel with him to Valletta and then go on to Gozo to see them. I've heard that the temples are constructed from some huge stones, similar to your own Stonehenge but even more ancient. The myth is that they were built by giants!"

"That sounds amazing!" chipped in Violet.

"We should all go and see them! Karolina will make the perfect guide to go with us!" said Robert, waving his wine glass about for emphasis as he spoke. "Who's up for it? We can go tomorrow!"

"Dear boy, we can't. Please remember, we are here to work and help Major Fleming."

"Don't be such a killjoy Ronald. Besides, you don't need me. I'm the radio wizard! Nothing for me to do here is there major?"

The major said nothing but studied Robert for a moment, before shaking his head.

"See! The magnificent major agrees that I'm not needed. Alex, you're still on leave. You can come too. Now who else is not

Murder on Malta

needed for the major's mission . . .?" His gaze travelled the table, passed over Maude for a second, then came to rest on Violet.

"I'd like to come," said Violet as if Robert had prompted her.

"No!" said Percy. "I won't allow you to go swanning off with them! I want you here with me."

"I want to go!" replied Violet stubbornly. "You're always trying to tell me what to do and what not to do. I can go to Gozo if I like! You complain I don't act educated. Well old temples sound educated, don't they?" Then a sneaky expression crossed her young face . . . "I can be company for Karolina. I can be her chaperone!"

Ronald spoke up again, "Really Robert, I don't think this is a good idea. I think . . . "

Robert turned aggressively on Ronald. "Ronald. Think about it. You want me to go and enjoy myself, don't you. You don't want me hanging around here, bored, bad tempered, nothing to do but gossip to people all day . . . "

Ronald sat silently looking at Robert for a second or too, then backed down, "Well alright, if you feel you are not needed here, then I suppose so," then looked away awkwardly, embarrassed.

"That's fixed then!" said Robert happily, "The four of us Violet, Karolina, Alex and myself will go tomorrow. Oh, I say Ronald, be a dear and get us a car will you! You'll do that for me won't you? That's a good chap!" Robert gave Ronald a contrived false smile that seemed to have more threat than pleasantness in it. Ronald looked away, reluctant to meet Robert's eyes.

Karolina looked at Alex to see what he thought about the plan. Alex shrugged. "If it's okay with you? What about it, Ronald, do you think I'm needed here?"

"Oh no dear boy!" said Ronald. "As I said, you are on well-deserved leave. We can spare you, at least for one day. I insist you run along and enjoy yourself tomorrow!"

When the final course of dinner was finished and cleared away and the waiters had left the room, Major Fleming rose and addressed his guests. "I'm afraid that we have some confidential business to discuss, so I must apologise to the ladies, but perhaps Miss Karolina and Mrs Osborne would be so kind as to withdraw to the lounge for a few moments. I promise we will conclude our business as soon as possible and join you there without delay."

Karolina was puzzled and very curious to know what this mysterious business was all about. She would dearly have loved to stay, but reluctantly, with good grace, she rose and smiled her assent. As Violet came around the table Karolina linked her arm through Violet's and said, "Come on Violet, we two girls will leave them to their stuffy old business and go and have a nightcap in the lounge."

As soon as they had left, Major Fleming seated himself and spoke to the remaining guests. "Thank you all for remaining, and before I go on, I would like to remind you that everything I'm going to say must be treated as confidential and secret. Firstly, let me introduce myself properly. As some of you may have guessed," he glanced at Alex, "I'm not a major in the military police. I'm actually an officer in the Secret Service Bureau. Some of you may also be wondering why we asked the Admiralty for a team of specialists in breaking enemy cyphers to be assigned to Malta? Some of you will perhaps already know the background to our request?" Then looking again at Alex, he said, "and some of you may know very little at all. So that we're all on the same page, I believe I need to start from the beginning." He took a deep breath, then continued, "Since the armistice, there has been a lot of political uncertainty around the Mediterranean. Many national boundaries have changed and many small cultures have picked up on the rallying cry of 'self-determination' and are demanding independence. I'm sure you've heard of the civil disturbances in different countries and Malta is no exception. There have been riots and even deaths here as well. A vocal group are demanding independence from Britain, even though Malta voluntarily became a protectorate within the British Empire over a hundred years ago. That was when, they asked us to help kick out Boney and the French invaders. There is some support for their independence back in London, but a lot of concern also. We are very worried that as small countries gain independence, that big fish are watching very carefully for those little fish to appear, with the hope of snapping them up and extending their territory. Malta also has a very strategic position, sitting in between the African coast and the southern tip of Italy. That makes it valuable to any country. Our intelligence leads us to believe that one such power has infiltrated the independence movement here with foreign agents and is attempting to foment violent revolt. Some visible evidence of that is a widespread leaflet and poster campaign spreading propaganda against us. Also, our Radiotelegraphic Service on the roof of the Auberge – that rather grand building you passed on your way from the harbour to the hotel - has intercepted some encrypted radio traff Direction finding equipment suggests the source may be a boat or a ship transmitting from different locations in the sea around Malta."

"Do you have any idea who that power is?" asked Ronald.

"We do. We suspect one organisation in particular. They are called the '*Italia Irredenta Movement*'. Their posters and leaflets are pushing the idea that Malta belongs to Italy, as does Nice, Savoy, some cities in Dalmatia and Corfu. This is proving to be very popular propaganda for the fascist party in Italy, who are led by a politician called Mussolini. They believe that after Italy swapped sides to join us during the war, Italy should have been rewarded with those territories."

"I wasn't even aware that Malta had been Italian," said Robert.

"Technically, it was Sicilian, but that was before it was given to the Knights of St. John in the fifteenth century by the Holy Roman Emperor, Charles V, and before Napoleon took it from the knights in the late eighteenth century."

"Any idea who is controlling the operation here in Malta?" asked Ronald.

Major Flemming paused for a second before answering him. "No. Our intelligence suggests that their operation is based here, in Valletta, but we don't know who, or where."

"What about pinpointing where the radio transmissions are coming from in Valletta?" suggested Alex.

Major Flemming nodded, before he replied, "Unfortunately, there are no transmissions from Malta itself. They presumably know that we could easily pinpoint the source and finding a two-way radio would be perfect evidence against them. No, they must have some other way of communicating to the ship and then the ship relays

Murder on Malta

those reports back to the fascists by coded radio messages." Turning to Ronald, he said, "If your team can decrypt those reports, it will tell us more about their operation here on Malta and hopefully identify where their headquarters is and who is controlling the operation here in Valletta. Tomorrow, I'll provide you with all the copies of the transmissions and some offices to work in. Until then, I suggest we re-join the ladies in the lounge."

Chapter 7

As they had walked arm-in-arm into the lounge, Violet looked up at Karolina. "I adore your gown Karolina!"

"Well thank you, Violet. Yours is lovely too."

Violet looked down at her own much less elegant but more revealing dress and sighed. "Percy is so cheap. He would never let me have enough money to buy a beautiful gown like yours. Where did you get it?"

"Paris. But it wasn't from one of the big expensive fashion houses. It was from a small boutique and very reasonable."

"Oh Paris! That's so exciting. You won't believe how boring it's been for me coming out here with Percy. We hardly ever go out and he only ever talks about who said what at work. Never about exciting things like clothes."

"Can't you talk to Maude about clothes and things?

"Maude?" Violet laughed, she's worse'n Percy! She knows nothing about clothes. And look how she does her hair! Trying to make herself look younger and more attractive! Can't make a silk purse out of a sow's ear, can you!"

Karolina thought that Maude had every right to try to make the best of her appearance. In the few exchanges of conversation Karolina had had with Maude, she'd seemed a pleasant and likable young lady. It seemed to her that Violet must have some other reason for disliking her. Could there have been something going on between Maude and Violet's husband? Karolina had not noticed any tension between them over dinner. Her curiosity piqued, she decided to pay more attention in future.

Karolina and Violet took a seat in the lounge and a smiling waiter quickly came over. He introduced himself as Georgio and asked if they would like to order food or something to drink?

"Karolina! Do you know of any of them new American cocktails that are all the rage! Could we have one of them, you suppose?"

"I don't see why not. How about a Manhattan?"

"Oooh yes. Let's try a Manhattan!"

Karolina ordered the drinks and the waiter departed. She decided to see what else she could learn about Alex's colleagues while they waited to be served.

"So do all the others work for the Admiralty like Alex, decoding the enemy's secret messages," said Karolina nonchalantly.

"Oh yes. They all do. We all came out here from London together in 1917 to set up a new office just to do that."

Karolina smiled to herself about how easy it had been to get confirmation of the nature of Alex's hush-hush work from this young lady. It really didn't inspire much confidence in her intelligence, or her ability to keep a secret.

The waiter arrived with the drinks and Karolina took a small sip of hers. "This is very good Georgio. You make a very good Manhattan." Georgio smiled in delight at the complement, before bowing to her and leaving them to enjoy their drinks.

Maude took a large sip of hers. "Ooh" This is lovely! Makes me feel very swish drinking a cocktail in a posh hotel lounge," she giggled.

"Does Maude also do the same work as the men? That's very unusual for a woman."

Violet's face changed to a sneer again at the mention of Maude's name. "I suppose she does, but I think she does it just so she can hang around the men all day."

"Oh really. Any one man in particular?" said Karolina, suddenly wondering if Maude had been attracted to Alex, before Karolina had met him. Not that she was worried if Alex had had girlfriends before he met her, she said to herself, then quickly added, not that she and Alex were anything other than travelling companions anyway.

"No," said Violet. "She threw herself at Robert when we first got out here, but Robert soon got tired of her. Robert likes to go out and spend his money having a good time. He prefers girls who are more exciting than the likes of Maude!"

Karolina was watching Violet's face as she said this and saw a smug smile spread across Violet's face. Maybe Maude hadn't been the only one to attract Robert's attentions. Before Karolina could learn any more, she saw the rest of the group arriving from the dining room, having finished their meeting. She and Violet stood up, Violet giggling as her husband approached with a disapproving look on his face. "Look Percy. I'm drinking cocktails! It's called a Manhattan! I think it's American you know. Why don't you have a cocktail Percy? It might cheer you up a bit," and she giggled again.

"I think you're cheerful enough for both of us," said Percy. "I have some very important work to do tomorrow. We need to go to our room now."

"Oh, don't be such a killjoy Percy," argued Robert. "Let's all go out on the town and have some fun. Let's go and find the nearest casino and lose a bit of money!"

"That may be your idea of fun Robert, but it's not mine," said Percy.

"Nor mine old boy!" agreed Ronald

"What about you two?" asked Robert looking at Karolina and Alex. "You look like a girl who knows how to enjoy yourself Karolina!" looking at her with what Karolina could only describe as a leer.

"No thank you Mr. Smith. Going with you to the casino doesn't attract me at all," and she turned to Alex and said, "How about you?"

Alex smiled at the way Karolina had refused Robert's invitation, leaving people to wonder whether it was the casino or Robert that didn't attract her? Turning to Robert said, "Looks like you're on your own old chap!"

"Well, you don't know what you all are missing," said Robert defiantly and with a little slur in his voice. "I shall see you all tomorrow." Turning his back on the group, he made his way across the lounge and with a slight stagger through the door to reception.

Maude also chose to follow. Addressing the group, but without actually meeting anyone's eyes, she mumbled that she thought that getting a good night's sleep before tomorrow was a good idea and nodding to no one in particular, followed Robert from the room.

Violet turned to her husband and querulously asked, "Why aren't we going to the casino with Robert!"

"You know very well why not!" replied Percy angrily. "You know I have trouble getting eight hours sleep a night and if nothing else, we don't have money to burn like that immoral libertine!"

"We could go and just watch" argued Violet sullenly.

"No! and that's an end to it!" and taking his wife firmly by the elbow he wished James, Ronald, Alex and Karolina a good night. As they left the lounge, Violet, carrying her cocktail glass in one hand, looked back over her shoulder at the rest of the group. Giggling, she pulled her arm away from Percy and gave the group a coy flirtatious little wave with just her finger tips, as she disappeared from view.

"Well, that just leaves the four of us then," remarked James. Turning to Karolina he said, "I don't know if you like music, but there's a rather good jazz club within easy walking distance of the hotel?" Turning to Alex and Ronald, he said, "I'd be happy to take you all there if you'd like? I know the owner well and we would be assured of a good table?"

"What do you think Karolina?" asked Alex.

"I think it might be fun."

"Well, you gay young things go and enjoy your music," said Ronald. "I'm getting too old to dance the night away and still be able to concentrate the next day. I'll follow the others up the old apples and pears and see you at breakfast tomorrow."

By way of explanation, Alex leaned in to Karolina and whispered "Apple and pears means stairs. Cockney rhyming slang."

Ronald finished saying goodnight to them all, kissing the back of Karolina's hand in the process then, as good as his word, turned and left the lounge.

Karolina said, "and I'll need to get a wrap if we're going out into the night air, I'll pop back to my room and be back down in one minute."

Murder on Malta

"And I need to find the Maître d' and settle the bill, I'll meet you both in the lobby," said James.

Alex and Karolina left the lounge for the lobby and Karolina continued up the stairs to her room. Alex looked around and decided to take a comfortable looking chesterfield away from the outside door, close to the reception desk. The hotel manager, Mr. Critchley was checking a new guest in. The guest was clean shaven with slicked back red hair. He was well dressed in a dark green tweed suit, that looked suitable to wear about town, but a little heavy for the warmth of Malta. He had matching expensive brown leather case and briefcase, with his name "Mr. W. Arrowsmith" embossed in gold one inch high letters on the briefcase. Mr. Critchley was addressing him, "Yes sir. We have held one of our best rooms for you, despite your ship being delayed. I will get the porter to escort you to your room now sir. If you are hungry, I am sure he will bring some food to your room."

The new guest's reply was lost to Alex when he was distracted by the sight of Robert hurrying down the stairs and across to the manager. He leant in close to the manager and appeared to talk urgently to him. As they talked, the doorman came into the lobby from outside and called out to all those in the lobby, "Carriage for Mr. Robert Smith!"

Robert interrupted his conversation with the manager to turn and call out to the doorman, "Change of plans. Don't need it," before turning back to Mr. Critchley. The doorman shrugged and went back outside. Alex wondered what had caused Robert's change of plans. Just then a porter came down the stairs and Mr. Critchley signalled him over. He gave the porter a room key and indicated the new guest, who had been standing close by, watching Robert and the manager talking. The porter picked up the new guest's luggage and led him off, up the stairs to his room, while the manager passed Robert a sheet of paper from behind the reception desk. Robert took the paper and fully engrossed in it, also followed the porter and guest up the stairs. Alex looked thoughtfully after them.

Just a minute later, Karolina came down the stairs now wearing an attractive knitted wrap around her shoulders and crossed the lobby to Alex. As Alex struggled to rise from the armchair, leaning heavily on his walking stick, James came out of the lounge and strolled across to them. "It's only a few hundred yards to the nightclub, but would you like me to get a carriage?" James asked Alex.

"No. I can manage," said Alex gruffly.

Smiling pleasantly, James said, "Okay then, follow me," and offering Karolina his arm made his way towards the door, with Alex following behind.

Chapter 8

    Major Fleming, with Karolina on his arm, led the way while Alex, feeling a little left out, limped along behind them. Fortunately for Alex, the major had been telling the truth and the nightclub was not too far away. They turned left outside the hotel and followed the street downhill until they saw twenty or thirty steps leading down from their street to the parallel street below. At the bottom of the steps, they turned right and walked a short distance until they stood in front of the nightclub 'Buco-Nel-Muro'. The major translated for them. "It means 'Hole-In-The-Wall' night club," and externally it lived up to its name. The nightclub backed onto the cliff face that supported the fortifications above it. The front of the nightclub was long and windowless, broken only by the entrance. The wall was finished in a pale-yellow stucco. Above the frontage a wrought iron railing ran the length of the building at the edge of a roof terrace. Alex recognised the row of blue and yellow flower pots lining the edge of the terrace and realised it was the building he had been looking down on from his bedroom window. The front entrance was a double arched door with two small coloured glass windows set high up in each door. One of the doors stood open to the street where a broad, heavily built, tough-looking man with dark skin and dark curly hair was slouched against the wall inside. He recognised the major, stood up straight and greeted him with a friendly "Good evening, Major Fleming. Are you dining with us this evening?"

    "No, Alessandro, I have just brought a couple of friends for drinks and to enjoy the music tonight. Do you have a nice table for us?"

"Of course Major Fleming. For you we will make sure there is a very nice table. Please follow me."

Alessandro led them down a darkly lit corridor that Alex realised must be a tunnel taking them inside the limestone cliff. They went down several steps to another set of double doors which he held open for them. He led them into a large luxuriously decorated cavern-like room. The nightclub had a stage at the far end, which was occupied at the moment by a jazz quartet playing a lively ragtime piece from before the war. In front of the stage the dance floor was busy with dozens of couples laughing and dancing vigorously to the music. Down either side of the large room were discreet booths capable of seating four to six people, but only a few of the booths were occupied. People seemed to prefer to be out in the open and enjoying the hustle and bustle with other customers. The arched ceiling was unexpectedly high and painted a dark blue with a magnificent candelabra lighting the stage and dancefloor. Each of the individual tables had one small discreet, heavily shaded table lamp. The floor under the tables and on the dancefloor was polished wood. Against the wall furthest from the stage was a long bar. The bar top itself was dark wood, the front edge of which was protected by a cushioned green leather bar rail. Behind the bar two white jacketed bartenders were quickly and professionally selecting and mixing drinks from the massive selection on the shelves behind them. Alessandro led them to one of the booths and asked, "Will this be satisfactory, Major Fleming?"

"This will be fine Alessandro," Major Fleming indicated one of the bench seats that faced the stage to Karolina and she slid in. The major followed and sat alongside her leaving Alex to take the opposite bench seat facing back towards the bar.

Turning to Karolina the major asked, "Do you like ragtime or jazz music Karolina?"

"Oh, I think I like both. Jazz is really taking over from ragtime, back home in America."

"These guys tonight are good. They're the club's house band and know how to keep everyone on the dance floor. This music is really good to dance to." Alex suspected that the major was intending to asking Karolina to dance and was secretly pleased when he was interrupted by the waitress coming to the table. She was wearing a black dress, showing an awful lot of décolletage. The dress ended about ten inches above her knees. Her legs were clad in dark stockings and she wore high stiletto-heeled shoes. Leaning in close to the major she said "Why Major Fleming, how nice to see you again! And I see you have some new friends with you." She gave Karolina a frozen smile and completely ignored Alex.

"Hello Coco. Nice to see you as well. May we have some drinks do you think?" Looking at Karolina then Alex he asked "How about martinis? Dry? Yes?" Receiving nods from both of them, he turned back to Coco. "Three dry martinis' please Coco."

"Yes sir, anything you want James," she said after giving him another sweet smile and Karolina another frosty one, before she left the table.

"You seem well known here James. Coco seems to know you especially well!" said Karolina with a knowing glance.

For the first time since Alex had met him, he thought the major looked a little embarrassed.

Murder on Malta

They settled back to listen to the music while they waited for their drinks, which Coco soon delivered. As they were enjoying their drinks, a beautiful tall slim woman, with long silky black hair came over to the table. She was wearing a glamourous black floor length dress decorated with glittering gold sequins. Looking down at Alex, she said in a dark husky voice, "Mind if I slide next to you . . . ?"

Alex quickly slid over and the young lady gracefully lowered herself into the booth. "Good evening Major Fleming. Always nice to see you here."

"Good evening, Maria. Nice to see you too. These are my friends Alex and Karolina."

Nodding to Karolina she turned to Alex to ask, "and are you also in the army Alex?"

Finding himself suddenly getting hot under the collar, he stuttered his reply, "No. No, Maria, I'm, I'm in the navy."

"Really . . . I find sailors *so* much more interesting than soldiers . . ." and fluttered her eyes at him. "Are you serving on HMS Warspite? I see she is back in Valletta harbour,"

"No, I'm afraid I have a boring job ashore."

"Oh, I'm sure it's not as boring as you say. What is it you do?"

"I just shuffle papers around. It really is very boring work you know."

Maria didn't seem to think Alex or his work were boring. In fact, she had shuffled a little closer to Alex as she was talking. He was grateful to Karolina when she stepped in and asked Maria, "What is it you do here Maria?"

Murder on Malta

Major Fleming answered before Maria could tear her eyes away from Alex, "Maria is the owner of the night club and she's also an extremely good singer. Will you be singing for us tonight, Maria?"

Still looking at Alex, Maria replied to the major, "Yes, in fact once this number finishes, I will be starting my set. I do hope you'll all stay and hear it."

"I'm sure we will," said the major.

Taking her eyes off Alex for the first time since she had arrived, she said, "Well I hope you all enjoy the show, settle back and have a few drinks." Maria slid her long legs out of the booth and rose. Blowing a kiss to Alex she turned and walked slinkily across the dance floor to the stage just as the band finished their number. Stepping up onto the stage she took the microphone from the stand and spoke into it in a low husky voice, "Hi everybody. I hope you're all having a great time tonight?" The audience responded with loud applause and cries of approval. "This next song is for all those new friends out there." Turning to the band she said "Okay boys, let's play some jazz . . . " and as the band began to play she looked across the room directly at Alex and began to sing in a low sensuous voice, "After you've gone, and left me cryin' . . . ."

More songs followed, all of which met with enthusiastic applause from the audience including James and Alex. Karolina seemed less enthused. The band and Maria went through a repertoire of ragtime blues and jazz songs. Coco frequently came to the booth to make sure that nobody had an empty glass and the evening went quickly until they were surprised to realise it was two a.m.

"Major, if you'll forgive me, I've had a long day. Would you mind if we called it a night?" requested Karolina.

"Of course not. I didn't mean to overtire you. I'll get the bill and we'll make our way back to the hotel." Signalling to Coco, the major soon settled up and they made their way out. Karolina found the night air to be cool and refreshing as they walked back towards the hotel. The major kept up a constant conversation with Karolina all the way back through the narrow streets and up the numerous steps. When they arrived at the hotel, Major Fleming accompanied them into the lobby. Karolina stood beside Alex and said, "Thank you, the music was fantastic and I've had a wonderful night. Do you have far to go now?"

"Not far," he said with a wide smile on his face showing his perfect white teeth. "About a ten-minute walk which on a night like this will be an absolute pleasure, just as the rest of this evening has been. I'll wish you all a good night." Then, looking directly at Karolina, he said in a softer more seductive voice, "I hope you enjoy your trip to the island of Gozo tomorrow. You know that duty prevents me from coming with you, but once the work is underway, I'd be happy to be your guide and show you some more of the beautiful sights that Malta has to offer. . . "

Karolina felt a little flustered by the handsome major's attentions and wasn't sure what to say to his offer. "Thank you major. You're very kind. I'll have to consider that after I've seen Gozo." For some reason she glanced across to Alex who was still standing next to her. He appeared to not be listening to their conversation, but studying a marble statue next to the door. With a casual salute to her and a quick nod to Alex, the major turned on his heel and walked briskly out into the night air.

Alex and Karolina walked slowly through the lobby and started to climb the stairs to their rooms. "What do you think of our Major Fleming?" asked Karolina.

Alex paused before replying. "I think he's probably quite a nice chap."

"Good looking, do you think?"

"Couldn't say," said Alex gruffly. He looked quickly at Karolina as she climbed the stairs alongside him and thought he caught a glimpse of a smile on her face before her expression switched to one of thoughtfulness.

"I would imagine he's very popular with the ladies," she mused.

Alex grunted.

"I wonder what beautiful romantic sites he's planning to take me to when I get back from Gozo?"

This time, when Alex glanced quickly at her, he could see she was definitely trying to hide her laughter. "You know, sometimes you can be too clever for your own good!" he said, as he joined in her laughter.

"Well, here's my room Alex. Thank you too for a wonderful night. I'd like to do it again and soon." Stepping closer she reached up and gave him a peck on the cheek before pausing when she realised that he wasn't actually paying any attention. A little affronted by this she asked "What's the matter?".

"Can you smell anything?" he asked, worriedly.

"Why. Did you forget to shower today."

"No. Seriously. That's smoke!"

They both looked up and down the corridor. Karolina was the first to spot a wisp of smoke coming from under a door, two rooms down.

Alex quickly stepped up to the door and banged hard on it with the handle of his walking stick. After a few seconds he shouted "Hello there! Open the door!"

When there was no answer he tried the handle, only to find it was locked. Raising his walking stick he banged on the door again and repeated his calls to open the door. When there was still no response after repeated attempts, Karolina said, "We need to break the door down!"

By now a plump and elderly gentleman with silver white hair and a bushy white moustache, had emerged from the room next door. He was clad in pyjamas and a Japanese style dressing gown, carrying a heavy walking stick with a brass handle. Looking at Alex and Karolina he said "What the devil's going on?"

Alex stopped banging on the door for a second to answer him. "I'm sorry sir, it looks like we may have a fire in here. Would you mind helping us break the door down?"

Seeing the wisp of smoke rising from underneath the door the elderly gentleman tied his dressing gown more securely around his waist. "Of course, young lad. Now miss, if you'll step back and let the hound see the fox, we'll have the door open in seconds!"

Together Alex and the elderly gentleman stepped back and studied the door while gathering their breath. "On three, me young fellah me lad!" exclaimed the gentleman, then without preamble shouted "THREE!" He and Alex charged at the door and hit it simultaneously. With a crash it collapsed inwards. The elderly gentlemen grabbed hold of the door frame to prevent himself from flying into the room. Alex was not so lucky. He flew through the open doorway, stumbling forward, unable to get his bad leg underneath him in time to prevent himself from falling full length into the room.

"My God!" exclaimed the elderly gentleman from the doorway. Alex knew it wasn't the smoke billowing from the smouldering armchair in the room that had caused the exclamation. Lying inches from Alex's face was the dead body of Robert Smith, blood seeping from underneath it!

Chapter 9

Alex was the first to recover. Smoke was now pouring vigorously from the armchair next to the bed and filling the room. He struggled awkwardly to his feet as quickly as he could. He looked around for something in which he could fetch water. Not seeing anything and also not seeing where his walking stick had fallen, he limped as quickly as he could into the room's bathroom. Still seeing no containers, he grabbed both the towels from the rack on the wall and pushed them into the sink. Turning both taps on full, he kneaded the towels in the splashing water until they were thoroughly soaked. By now Karolina was at the door to the bathroom. She had retrieved his walking stick from where it had fallen and was watching what he was doing. "Here! Throw these over the fire," Alex instructed her, passing the towels to Karolina and receiving his walking stick in return. Karolina turned and in two swift steps was at the smoking chair. She threw the soaking towels over the source of the smoke and within seconds the fire seemed to be out, although the room was still filled with smoke.

A round of clapping sounded from the door way. The elderly gentleman stood there, applauding, having watched everything, "I say. Jolly good team work. Do this sort of thing for a living do you? You could you know. Go on the stage, what! Fellah on the floor doesn't look so good though. Not part of the act?"

"No sir," replied Karolina, bending down to examine Robert more closely, "Not part of the act at all. I'm afraid he's dead."

"Nothing much I can do then," said the elderly gentleman. "I'll be off to the bar then for a snifter or two. Most excitement I've had

Murder on Malta

since Freddie Figgis's Golden Labrador ran off with General Chumberley-Futton's wooden leg." So saying, the elderly gentleman in the kimono and carpet slippers shuffled off along the corridor.

"Re-assure me Alex," said Karolina, "this is a hotel, isn't it, not a home for the mentally insane?"

"It is a hotel, Karolina, but the guests are mostly English, so it's easy to get confused. But we have other things to worry about now. If I hold the fort here, could you go and get the manager to come up here. We also need to get hold of Major Fleming as soon as possible."

"I suppose there's no doubt is there? Robert was murdered."

"No doubt at all."

After Karolina had gone, Alex struggled to lift the door from the floor and propped it roughly into the door frame. While waiting for the manager, Alex made a careful examination of the room. Robert's suitcase had been emptied onto the floor and the case thrown carelessly into a corner. Clothes were in an untidy sprawl covering much of the carpet. His briefcase had been tipped out on the bed and lay on top of the contents. A large amount of blood had pooled on the floor under Robert's facedown body. Drawers hung open and empty. Wardrobe doors were opened wide and the wardrobe also stood empty. Alex carefully lifted the soaking towels from the armchair. The seat cushion was a sodden blackened mess, with the stub of a cigar stub resting on top of it. Alex noted the ashtray still poised on the arm of the chair and the thick line of cigarette or cigar ash still in the ashtray. He made a guess that the fire had been started when Robert's still burning, unattended cigar had been balanced on the edge of the ash tray. As the end of the cigar burned and turned to ash, eventually the remaining stub would have overbalanced and fallen from the ashtray into the chair. Looking at the wastepaper basket at the side of the chair, Alex realised they'd been lucky. If the cigar had fallen that way, the crumpled brown paper in the wastepaper basket would have ignited a much more vigorous fire. The room light was off and the bedside light was on, but there were no signs that Robert had been to bed yet. As Alex was making a cursory examination of the bathroom there was a timid knocking on the remains of the door. Alex slid the door to the side to see the manager standing there with a look of panic and horror on his face.

"Miss McAllister said there had been a murder! I've never heard of such a thing. This is terrible." Peering around Alex's shoulder, the manager caught a glimpse of the state of the room and much to his horror, the head and shoulders of the body. "Oh my God. Oh my God. Whatever shall I do? All my guests will leave! I'll never be able to let this room again!"

"Mr. Smith isn't doing so well either," said Alex flatly. "Did you send for Major Fleming?"

"Yes. Yes, I sent the boy. Told him to run as fast as he could."

"Well until he gets here, I'll stay in here and will keep the door closed. I suggest you get a porter to stand in the corridor and keep other guests away from this room." Alex nodded to the small crowd of guests now stood in the hallway. Judging by the fact that they were mostly still in their nightclothes, he assumed they had been woken by the commotion. Now they were clustered outside the door, trying to see into the room.

"Yes of course. Good idea. I will do that straight away." Finally able to tear his eyes away from the body he turned away and left. Alex was just about to slide the broken door back in place when Karolina squeezed through.

"Are you okay with this," asked Alex, nodding towards the body.

"Of course!" she replied. "Seems a bit like old times doesn't it."

Alex smiled. Karolina had surprised him when they had first met, both with her confidence and then by how nothing seemed to throw her. So unlike the few English girls 'of breeding' that he'd met.

"How did he die?"

"I don't know yet. Didn't think it was a good idea to move the body until Major Fleming arrives. Could be stabbed. Could be shot."

"Shot! Someone would have heard that surely."

"Not if they had used a silencer," replied Alex, "Our friends in the espionage business have been using silencers since before the war. I've heard the British Secret Service have a preference for the one made by Mr. Maxim."

"You think it might have been a spy then?" asked Karolina

"It's too early to rule it out yet, but why would they pick Robert out? We need more information," replied Alex as he carefully scanned the hotel room from where he stood.

"Has your inner Sherlock Holmes kicked in yet? Noticed any clues?"

"Afraid not. Except it looks like the source of the fire was one of Robert's cigars falling into the armchair. Could have been a lot worse."

They stood there in silence for several minutes, each studying the scene, until finally there was another knock on the remains of the door. Alex slid it aside to admit Major Fleming.

As Karolina started to speak, he held up a finger for silence and continued to examine the scene in detail. Eventually he said. "Okay. Lieutenant Armstrong, would you oblige me in helping me to turn the body over please."

Together they bent and, as respectfully as they could, turned Robert Smith onto his back.

James studied the body for a moment before saying, "Single stab wound to the chest. Would have entered the heart. No chance of survival. He would have died immediately." Carefully pulling the fabric of Robert's shirt straight and then examining the hole in it, he straightened up and said, "Not a normal knife. Thin bladed, a weapon made for stabbing not cutting. Something like a stiletto, flick knife or a Scottish dirk."

He scanned the room carefully one last time, then turning to Alex and Karolina said, "I'll leave the porter on guard outside the door. My sergeant will be here soon and he'll take over. In the meantime, I suggest we reconvene to more salubrious surrounds, in the room where we all had dinner earlier. I would like to ask you a few questions."

They left the room and stopped to talk to the porter on guard outside. He was talking to two elderly women in dressing gowns and one fully dressed guest, who Alex had noted checking into the hotel earlier that night. The major gave the porter strict instructions that nobody was to enter the room and that his sergeant would take over from him soon. Together the major, Alex and Karolina descended to the ground floor, where the major led them into the bar. "Lieutenant Armstrong, I don't think it would be inappropriate to have a stiffener before we start. I think I'll have a brandy. How about you, Lieutenant?"

"A brandy would be most welcome."

"And you Miss McAllister? Perhaps a sherry to steady your nerves?"

"There is nothing unsteady about my nerves, major, however, I don't see why I shouldn't have a brandy too."

"What ho! Brandies all round, is it? Don't mind if I do! Mines a large one. Saves all that running backwards and forwards!" The voice came from the end of the bar where the plump elderly man with the bushy moustache and the kimono was ensconced.

"Good evening, Lieutenant-Colonel Pinkersley. I'm afraid I didn't see you there sir," said Mayor Fleming.

"Good evening, sir," said Karolina. "Thank you so much for your help earlier."

"Think nothing of it me gal. Glad to be of service to you young things. Y'can call on me any time, you know." The bar tender placed the colonel's glass of brandy in front of him and the colonel picked it up and he raised it in toast to her and James.

Drinks in hand Major Fleming led them from the bar to the private dining room, he said "So it appears you've met Lieutenant-Colonel Pinky Pinkersley?"

Karolina replied, "Yes, he helped us to break Robert's door down." She paused for a second considering what to say, then decided to be blunt. "Is the colonel . . . well, as we would say back home, . . . one brick short of a full load?"

Major Fleming looked at her and laughed. "Is he crazy you mean? Well, we prefer to say that he's 'a little bit eccentric'. He's also a marine and highly decorated at that. Fought in the Great War, the Boer War and several other wars and campaigns." He laughed. "If you have the time, get him to tell you about how he personally won the Zanzibar War. Apparently, the whole war lasted just thirty-nine minutes. He'll tell you that he'd barely time to finish his pre-war tot of rum! Of course, it will take him twice as long as the war lasted to tell you about it and you'll have to keep his glass full while he's telling you!"

They entered the private dining room and the major closed the door behind him. Now in private his attitude became decidedly more businesslike. "Please sit down, both of you. Starting from when I left you, I would like you to tell me everything that happened tonight. Please do not spare any detail. Lieutenant Armstrong, perhaps you would go first?"

Alex quickly and concisely related the experiences of this evening, with Karolina occasionally butting in where she felt Alex had missed something, or not been clear on a detail. Major Fleming listened intently, only interrupting twice to ask clarifying questions. When Alex reached the end of the story, he sat quietly for a few moments. Karolina took the opportunity to ask the major, "Will you be fingerprinting the room, James? I don't think I touched anything, but I'm happy to let you take my fingerprints for elimination purposes."

James smiled at her, "Regretfully Karolina, although I know fingerprinting has proved valuable to the American and British police forces, the technology is yet to reach Malta."

Murder on Malta

Major Fleming sat thoughtfully, studying the pair closely for several minutes without talking. Alex met his scrutiny without comment, without expression. Karolina suffered his inspection for a minute or two, then burst out, "Look, do you think we're hiding something! Do you think we're involved in some way? I would have thought in your line of business you would have been a better judge of character than that! What apparent motive do you think we might have for stabbing Robert Smith to death!"

With a sigh, Major Fleming sat back. "No, Miss McAllister, I do not think of either of you as suspects. I don't just base that upon my ability to judge character which as it happens is actually quite good. However, I also accept that in the espionage business being able to conceal your character is also pretty much a pre-requisite. You might call it, in Mr Darwin's words, 'a survival characteristic'. And as for an apparent motive, until I conduct my investigation, I would point out that no one as yet has an apparent motive. No Miss McAllister, I base my trust in your innocence not on my judgement of character, but on a couple of facts. You appear to have a reliable witness in Lieutenant Colonel Pinkersley, even if he is sometimes as mad as a box of frogs. He saw you breaking down Robert Smith's bedroom door and your subsequent discovery of the body. Secondly, based on the coagulation of the blood, he had died at least an hour or so earlier. Therefore, at a time of the murder you have an alibi. An alibi supported by another reliable witness, in this case, myself. No, Miss McAllister, I was not thinking about your character or your possible motives."

Switching tack, Major Fleming said, "As well as being a judge of character, I am also naturally curious and I asked for and received a copy of your statements to the police concerning the murder you solved on Crete. Quite a professional job and a very observant performance if I may say so."

Here again the major paused, weighing up the two young people in front of him.

Studying both of them closely he said "Considering the secret nature of the work we are involved in here, and the fact that the murderer may well be a foreign agent, this investigation will fall under my jurisdiction. This gives me a problem. Not just in terms of workload. Some of the people I must investigate are female. In fact, two females, excluding yourself that is Miss McAllister. I think I would appreciate your help Miss McAllister, both as a chaperone and also as an observer during my interviews. I believe your unique female perspective on their responses would be invaluable. Lieutenant Armstrong, since I am equally convinced of your innocence, I would also greatly appreciate your help and observations regarding the people I must investigate. Will you both offer me your help?"

"Of course, major. We will help in any way we can," replied Alex.

"Thank you, both of you." said Major Fleming rising. "In that case I suggest we all get as much sleep as we can. I will take care of the formalities with the body and have some more men here in the morning. I will requisition this room for interviews starting after breakfast tomorrow. Thank you once again for your help."

Murder on Malta

Chapter 10

The next morning Karolina was surprised to realise she must have fallen asleep soon after returning to her room. Unfortunately, despite the late night, she awoke at her normal hour resulting in her only having a few hours' sleep. Falling back asleep was impossible, as she immediately came fully awake; her mind turning over the happenings of the previous night. Giving up her fruitless attempts to stop her brain churning through the events, she got dressed and went down to breakfast. As she entered the breakfast room the only person she recognised was Violet, who sat at a table for two by herself. From the looks of her reddened eyes Karolina thought she must have been crying.

Approaching the table Karolina asked, "Is Mr. Osbourne perhaps not coming down for breakfast today?"

"No," she replied trying to still a sob. "He's still asleep and doesn't take breakfast anyway. He says it upsets his stomach. That doesn't stop him having to have his coffee in the morning though," she said resentfully, before stopping and looking up at Karolina. "Have you heard the dreadful news? Robert was murdered in his room last night! William on reception told me!" This time she couldn't hold back the sobbing and pulled out her handkerchief to dry her eyes.

Karolina sat down at the table opposite her and reached across the table to take hold of one of her hands. "I'm so sorry Violet. You really liked him, didn't you?"

"I thought he was really nice. He always used to talk to me and tell me how pretty I looked. He used to go out dancing and to the casinos and was always trying to get me to go with him, but of course I couldn't because of Percy."

"Did Robert go to the casinos a lot?"

"Quite a lot. He told me he liked to play baccarat. He used to say he was very good at it and had a foolproof way to win and that one day he'd be a millionaire." She sniffed some more, then continued, "but I don't think he really was very good at it. Often, the day after going to the casinos, he would be in really bad mood because he'd lost a lot of money."

"But you never went with him to the casinos?"

"No, but I'd have loved to. All those beautiful ladies in their expensive clothes and jewels. Robert said he'd buy me some jewellery to wear if I went with him, but I never did get the chance."

"When he left after dinner last night, he said he was going to the casino. Did he ask you to go with him?"

Suddenly, Violet stopped her sobbing and looked up from her handkerchief that she was screwing up in her hands. She looked directly at Karolina. "Why are you asking? Why do you want to know?" she said suspiciously.

Karolina squeezed Violet's hand again. "It's important we find out everything we can, to help that nice attractive Major Fleming to find Robert's killer."

"Major Fleming is investigating it then?" Violet paused in thought.

"Oh, I'm sure of it, what with the secret nature of Robert's work. You know what the military are like. They won't stop until they find out who killed Robert."

"I'd like to help Major Fleming," said Violet thoughtfully, "but nothing I know will be of any help."

"Well, do you know if he was carrying anything valuable? He may have been robbed."

"Oh, he was very rich. He said he was very clever buying the right stocks and shares and things. He said he'd made a lot of money last year. He said that he was going to buy a brand-new expensive motorcar when he got home and he was going to take me for rides in the countryside. He was going to buy a swanky house in a posh part of London." Violet seemed to brighten up remembering what he had said and stared into space thinking about it. Suddenly her eyes came into focus and looking behind Karolina, she said "Mr. Armstrong, have you heard the terrible news?"

"Yes, Violet. How are you bearing up?"

"It's horrible Mr. Armstrong. Miss McAllister says that poor Robert was robbed!"

Karolina corrected her, "I said it was a *possibility* that he may have been robbed Violet. Major Fleming will find out. He'll want to talk to all of us to help him."

"Yes Miss McAllister. I'll help however I can."

"Okay, Violet, now Lieutenant Armstrong is giving me looks like he could eat the north end of a south bound steer, so I'm going to take him and get him some breakfast. If you start feeling upset or want someone to talk to then find me and I'll do what I can for you."

"Thank you, Miss McAllister, You're a real angel, a proper lady!"

Karolina rose and moving away with Alex following found a table away from Violet where they could sit and talk privately.

Alex looked at Karolina. "So, what did you find out from Violet?"

"What makes you think I found anything out?"

Alex smiled and said nothing.

"Well, it sounds like Robert was in the process of seducing the poor girl and she'd fallen head over heels for him but I could have told you that last night at dinner. When it comes down to it, I think she'd fall for any man who gave her a second glance." She stared hard at him. "Alex?" She continued to look meaningfully at Alex, waiting for him to respond.

"What? Oh. No. Not me. She seemed nice, but I never . . . well you know . . . I mean she's married. I never really talked to her."

"I will believe you for the time being, but beware, I do have my eye on you!"

The waiter approached their table and Karolina recognised him from last night. She greeted him cheerfully, "Good morning Georgio, what can you offer us for breakfast?"

"Good morning Miss McAllister," Georgio smiled at her and handed her the menu. They each studied the menu for a minute. Karolina was surprised to see that even in Malta she could order a traditional English Breakfast of bacon, egg, tomatoes mushrooms and fried bread. They both decided that would be just the thing to restore their energy, and both ordered the full English breakfast together with strong coffee for Karolina and what Alex called 'Builders Tea' for himself. When Georgio had gone, Karolina continued to describe her conversation with Violet. "Apparently, he enjoyed a bit of a gamble. Seems he may not have been very good at it. Lucky he was quite wealthy."

"Yes," replied Alex. "He inherited his money from a rich uncle who died a year or two back."

"Not according to what he told Violet. He told her that he was a genius on the stock market. Made a killing last year."

"Interesting. Did you find out anything else?"

Karolina recounted her conversation with Violet from the night before and from this morning, pausing only when the waiter arrived with their breakfasts. They had almost finished eating when Major Fleming entered the breakfast room. He was closely followed into the room by Sergeant Moore. Major Fleming looked very smart and handsome in his crisp uniform, carrying a swagger stick and a notebook under his arm. Considering his lack of sleep, he looked alert and energetic as he walked briskly across the room to them.

"Good morning, Lieutenant Armstrong, Karolina. Well rested and well fed, I hope?"

"Good morning, James," replied Karolina. "Well fed certainly. I'm as well rested as you could hope for on about three hours of sleep."

"My apologies for that. I'm afraid a full night's sleep would be a luxury considering the circumstances. I have requisitioned the same private room to use as a base for our work and asked for some strong coffee to be delivered there. If you'd like to join me there when you both finish your breakfasts, perhaps the coffee will awaken you?"

Karolina looked across at Alex, who nodded. She replied for both of them, "We'll come with you now James," and rising from her chair she waited for Alex, as he positioned his walking stick to support his weight before rising with difficulty to follow the major and the sergeant from the room.

Chapter 11

The four of them settled themselves in the private room where Major Fleming took a seat at the head of the table. Turning to his sergeant he said, "Sergeant Moore, be so good as to go to Miss Maude Cooper's room and inform her that I'd like a word with her in here as soon as possible, then escort her down here." As the sergeant departed on his errand, the major opened his notepad and addressed Karolina and Alex. "When I start an investigation, I like to make a list of things I know, as well as listing things I don't know. Last night you both gave me a very good description of what happened, but I'd like to start by asking Lieutenant Armstrong for his opinion on Robert Smith?"

"Well, I wouldn't say I knew the man very well. He tended to work a lot by himself. His job was working with radio equipment to intercept enemy messages. That meant he spent a lot of time travelling by himself to the various radio receiving stations." Alex paused for thought before continuing. "He didn't mix well with the rest of the team. Seemed to have a chip on his shoulder about not being as academically qualified as they are – although the Lord knows - I have no academic qualifications, and he wasn't chummy with me either. He seemed to me to be a bit of a charmer, a lady's man. I'd heard Ronald describe him as a 'libertine and a scoundrel'. He didn't like him at all. Come to think of it, Percy didn't like Robert either. Percy felt Robert paid much too much attention to Violet and Percy was jealous of the way Violet responded.

Karolina chipped in, "That seemed to be reaching a head. Robert had asked Violet out several times, but apparently without her accepting, but her agreeing to go on this trip to Gozo looked like causing a major row."

Major Fleming was nodding and taking notes. "Anything else I should know about the victim?" he asked Alex

Karolina answered, "He enjoyed the high life, gambling and dancing. He tried to give the impression he had a lot of money, but he also lost a lot gambling. He was also not very clear about explaining where he got the money from. It would be interesting if you could find out if he did actually have a lot of money or if he was just spinning a line to Violet?"

"You suspect he may have been murdered for the money?" asked the major.

"Well, the room was searched after all. Maybe he interrupted someone going through his room and then there was a fight," said Karolina.

"The room was searched after he was killed, not before," said Alex.

"Why do you say that Lieutenant," said Major Fleming looking at Alex quizzically.

"The blood was on the floor, underneath the clothes that had been emptied out of his suitcase," said Alex matter-of-factly.

"Interesting," said Major Fleming, studying Alex more closely than he had up to now. "I had actually missed that in my examination of the room."

"Of course, we don't know for sure if the search of the room was genuine," said Karolina thoughtfully. "It may have been a deliberate ploy to make us think that robbery was the motive so we didn't look for any other sort of motive."

"Also," added Alex. "It looked like he hadn't unpacked anything, there were no personal possessions on the table or the chest of drawers. Nothing in the wardrobe or the bathroom."

Major Fleming put his pen down decisively on his note pad and looked at the young pair. "Are you sure that you two are not professionals? Maybe you're working for my competition? Perhaps the American Bureau of Investigation?"

Karolina looked across at Alex for a second then back at the major. "I can promise you James that we are just who we say we are. We just seem to work well as a team, that's all. Alex is good at spotting small details and I'm good at the thinking. He's the eyes, so I have to be the brain!" She stared challengingly at Alex, until he burst out laughing.

"Well, I think you're both going to prove very helpful to me."

At that moment, there was a knock on the door and the sergeant entered. "Miss Cooper to see you, as ordered sir."

Maude Cooper entered the room and quickly glanced at the three of them sat at the table. She came into the room and hesitantly took a place at the table next to Karolina. She placed her hands together on the table and looking down at her hands rather than up at anyone's face, before saying "Yes Major Fleming? How can I help?"

"Thank you for coming down so quickly Miss Cooper," said Major Fleming, then waited in silence for some seconds before continuing. "Are you aware of the incident that took place in this hotel last night?"

"No major. When I left the group after dinner I went to my room. I was in the process of getting dressed this morning when your sergeant knocked on my door and told me you had summoned me here."

"Well Miss Cooper, I am afraid I have some bad news for you. Early this morning, one of your colleagues was discovered to have died."

"No! Who on earth was it!" exclaimed Maude.

"It was Robert Smith, I'm afraid, Miss Cooper"

For a few seconds, Maude Cooper's expression froze, then, gradually it crumpled before she completely dissolved into heartrending sobs. She cried out, "No! it Can't be! He can't be dead!" before her sobbing became so bad that her words became unintelligible.

"Perhaps gentlemen, you could leave Miss Cooper with me for a few minutes," suggested Karolina, moving closer to Maude and putting her arm around her shoulders. Major Fleming and Alex nodded to each other then rose and together with the sergeant left the room.

Karolina consoled Maude for several minutes, letting her sob onto her shoulder, until finally Maude started to regain her composure. "You must have really liked Robert," she said.

"Yes! He was wonderful! I loved him!"

"I hadn't realised you were that close."

"Robert used to insist we kept it secret. He said they wouldn't let us work together if they found out, so he never showed me any affection when we were in public."

"Had you known him long?"

"Yes. We knew each other in England and then when we came out here, he was so attentive to me. He would tell me I was beautiful and that he loved me. No one else has ever said that to me!"

"I'm so sorry for you my dear. Where you planning to get married?"

"Yes. Well, we were. He said we had to wait until we got back to England before we could tell anyone, but then that trollop turned his head!

"Trollop?"

"Yes, that trollop Violet! She's a married woman, but that didn't stop her fluttering her eyes at my Robert! She turned his head! Last night, as we were going back to our rooms, I caught up with him at the reception desk. I asked him not to go on that trip to Gozo with her, but he just laughed and said there was nothing to worry about. That he wasn't serious about her. It was just a bit of fun! But when I started to cry, he told me he couldn't stand emotional women. He said it was my fault for being so clingy and now he needed some time to think about what he wanted to do when we got back to England. He was horrible to me! I think he was going to break off our relationship!"

Maude's sobbing resumed again and Karolina stopped her questioning and just concentrated on consoling her. After sometime, the sobbing started to ease and Karolina suggested that she escort Maude back to her room to rest.

When she returned from Maude's room to the private dining room, the sergeant was just showing Percy into the room, where James and Alex were helping themselves to coffee. Walking around

Murder on Malta

the table to sit next to Alex, Karolina also reached for the coffee pot and helped herself.

Percy was looking disapprovingly at her. "If we are going to be discussing sensitive Admiralty business, I object to the young lady being present."

Major Fleming looked at Percy sternly. "I have no intention of discussing your work, Mr Osborne. I am afraid we have something else, more serious to discuss." Percy looked worriedly from the major to Alex, before the major continued, "are you aware that a serious incident took place, last night, in this hotel?" Karolina was interested to note that James had used very similar wording when breaking the news to Maude. No hint of what sort of incident, or who had been involved. He was obviously waiting to study the reaction he got, when he announced Robert's death.

"I am not sir," said Percy stiffly. "As I think you are aware, my wife and I retired after dinner and I slept solidly throughout the night, until your sergeant here, " and he nodded towards the sergeant, "made a tremendous din, banging on my hotel room door!"

"Couldn't wake the gentleman, sir. Though how he could sleep through his own snoring's beyond me. Could 'ere it int' corridor!"

"Really!" Percy said, "I object . . . "

James interrupted him. "Your colleague, Robert Smith was found dead this morning."

Percy's mouth fell open and he stopped in mid complaint. After a second or two his mouth opened and closed a few times, without a sound coming out. Eventually he recovered enough to say "Dead! You're sure?"

"One doesn't like to make a mistake about such things, so we did double check," said James with a touch of irritation.

"Yes, well, of course you did, I'm sure. Really, I had no idea . . . Of course, I'm very sorry to hear that."

"Are you?" asked James. "Strikes me you and he didn't get along to well?"

"I didn't like the man. I thought he was a braggart and a philanderer, but I wished him no harm. Wait! How did he die?"

"I'm afraid to say he was murdered."

"Ha! I should have known! I bet he upset one husband too many and suffered the consequences! I could have foreseen something of the sort would happen to him," he said almost triumphantly.

"You would seem to fall quite well into the category of husbands that he upset," stated James.

"Hold on! You don't suspect me, do you! I would never do such a thing! There's many a time I could have given the man a good thrashing, but I'm too much of a gentleman. Kill a man! I would never do such a thing!"

"Can you tell us where you were last night?"

"I've already told you. After we left you last night, my wife and I went to our room and slept until your sergeant woke us up. My wife can vouch for me."

"I met your wife down here in the breakfast room some time ago Mr. Osborne. Did you not notice she had risen and left the room?" asked Karolina.

"What? Well, I suppose she must have woken earlier. I sleep very soundly. I have to take a sleeping draft. If I don't get enough sleep, I can't concentrate on the very difficult and demanding work I have to do."

"So, you can't say for sure that she was with you all of last night?" asked Karolina.

"Of course, she was! Where else could she have been?" then Percy clamped his mouth shut as all those in the room contemplated the most obvious answer to that question.

"Well thank you for being so helpful Mr. Osborne. I suggest you get yourself some breakfast. Despite this incident, we still have the work to do that I outlined to you all last night. Once I have interviewed Mr. Findlay, I would like to escort you all over to the military headquarters, where the necessary materials will have been setup for you to examine." The major nodded to his sergeant to escort Percy Osborne out and asked him to find and bring Ronald Findlay to the room.

Once the door had closed behind the sergeant and Percy, Karolina asked innocently, "Do you think the murder may have been connected to the decryption work that you want the team to do?"

Major Fleming, met her gaze expressionlessly and said just as innocently, "What decryption work are you talking about Miss McAllister."

With a smile Karolina said, "I'm afraid there is not much kept secret once Mrs. Osborne knows about it. She may have let slip something about Robert's mission here to other people. Do you think that may have led to his death?"

"It's quite possible that the people we're trying to catch would resort to violence and even murder, if they felt it necessary. They have already incited riots, which have led to civilian deaths, so yes,

I think there might possibly be a link. But, from what we've heard so far, my money is on it being tied into that love triangle. It's a motive that's as old as time itself."

Karolina was disappointed that she hadn't been able to trick James into satisfying her curiosity about the work that Alex was involved in. Her disappointment turned to concern however when she realised that if the work was responsible for Robert's death, then Alex might also be in danger.

"James, before we move on, I need to let you know that Violet wasn't the only young lady that Robert was involved with. Maude told me that he had been involved with her since she had arrived from Britain. She had been under the impression that they would be married on their return until last night when he disabused her of the notion. I'm starting to agree with Mr. Osborne's opinion of Mr. Smith, that he was a complete rat!"

At that moment, her thoughts on Robert's failings were cut short by a sharp knock on the door and Ronald Findlay was shown in.

"Sergeant, organise a couple of carriages to be waiting to take us to headquarters in half an hour or so, after I've finished talking to Mr. Findlay. Mr. Findlay, please take seat."

"Good morning, James, Alex. Good morning, Karolina, you're looking very sweet today" said Ronald, smiling widely before he sat down, "How can I help you, James?"

Karolina waited to see how James would break the bad news to Ronald.

James smiled at him and then said, "Good morning, Ronald. I hope your room is to your satisfaction?"

Murder on Malta

"Oh yes dear boy. I have a beautiful view of the harbour. It looks quite lovely."

"Good. I'm glad to hear it. I wondered if you could be a big help to me. I suppose you've heard already about the incident in the hotel last night?"

"No, whatever happened?"

"I'm afraid Robert Smith is dead."

Ronald continued to smile at James for several seconds with the smile on his face frozen. "I'm sorry. What did you say?"

"I'm afraid Robert Smith is dead."

"Dead. How can that be? He looked to be in perfect health. How can he be dead?" He showed no emotion other than puzzlement.

"I'm afraid his health had nothing to do with it. He was murdered."

Still Ronald's only response seemed to be puzzlement. "Murdered? But how? Do we know who did it?"

"No Mr. Findlay. We don't know who did it yet, but I can assure you that whoever did will be tracked down and punished. Do you know of any reason why someone would kill Mr. Smith?"

The puzzlement vanished from Ronald's face and was replaced by a guarded look for a few seconds, before he answered, "No. No reason at all. He was a lovely boy. We all loved him. What a terrible thing to happen."

"Forgive me Mr. Findlay, but having talked to some of your party, Robert Smith was definitely not universally liked."

"Well no. I suppose there was some friction between him and Percy, but you know, boys will be boys. There's always a bit of competition, a bit of jealousy between young men. Young bulls locking horns. You know what it's like."

"I understand he also liked to gamble?"

"Yes, I do believe that might be right but I didn't pry into his private life. We never mixed socially you know. That wouldn't have been the thing, what with me being his superior."

"With you being his superior, some people would think that it was your job to know what he was doing in his private life. Something like gambling can easily lead to debt and debt can lead to blackmail and in the sort of work that he does, being potentially open to blackmail is a very serious problem."

Ronald looked suddenly very shaken by James's words and struggled to say anything for several moments. Eventually he pulled himself together and tried to reassure James. "Oh no. I don't think there was any chance of debt with poor Robert. You may not know but he was actually quite wealthy."

"Do you have any idea of where that money came from, Mr. Findlay?"

"Oh, he never discussed that sort of thing with me. But someone did tell me they thought he sold some property for a large sum."

"Thank you, Mr. Findlay. As his direct superior, we are reliant on you to tell us anything that might help us with our investigation. Do you know of any reason at all that someone might want to kill Mr. Smith? Anything to do with his personal life, or his work? Anything at all?"

Ronald looked nervously from James, to Karolina and then to Alex. Looking about him as if to see if anyone could overhear, he said in a whisper, "I do know that when we were in Italy, he was interviewed by the Italian secret police . . . They asked to interview him and London said it was OK. They didn't tell me what it was about and nothing ever came of it, but he was questioned by them about an investigation they were conducting."

"Did you find out from Mr. Smith what the investigation was about?"

"No. I did ask him, but he said it was confidential and he couldn't discuss it with me. When I asked London, they said it was purely an Italian matter and I wasn't on the list of those that needed to know about it."

"Thank you, Mr. Findlay. You've been quite helpful," said James, closing his notebook.

"Oh, you are quite welcome dear boy. Anything I can do; you only have to ask you know."

"Well, unfortunately Robert Smith's death is not the only problem we have to deal with. Could I ask you to assemble your team in the lobby in a quarter of an hour or so? I have arranged for carriages to take us to headquarters, where I would like work to begin on decrypting the radio communications of the foreign agents."

"Of course, dear boy, we'll all be there waiting for you."

"Actually, I'm not sure if Maude will be up to it," said Karolina, "She was pretty upset."

"I really don't mind helping out under the circumstances," volunteered Alex. "You're short-handed and I'd be happy to help."

"Would you dear boy. That's so good of you. If you're absolutely sure you don't mind. I'm sure we're all terribly upset and will have difficulty concentrating, so it would be so good of you." So saying, Ronald Findlay rose from his chair and thanked the major before leaving the room.

"Comments?" asked James of Alex and Karolina.

Karolina had no hesitation, "Robert was a rat. Lower than a snake's belly. He was trying to seduce Violet and at the same time had proposed to Maude. If I'd have known of how he treated those two girls, I could have killed him!"

"Is that a confession Miss McAllister?" asked James with a broad smile on his face.

"Of course not! Just an expression of my disgust regarding how men treat women!"

"In our defence Miss McAllister, I think Mr. Robert Smith was not a fair example of men in general," argued James.

"Yes. Well. I'm just saying nobody had better treat me like that!" said Karolina, glaring at the two men in the room with her.

"I'm sure we would never dream of it," said James smiling at Karolina, "but getting back to the investigation, who do you think had a motive to kill Robert?"

"Percy is the most obvious suspect. He was obviously aware of the intrigue going on between Robert and Violet. While nothing seems to have actually happened between them, yet, Percy may have finally reached breaking point and attacked Robert. But with a knife? I can't see Percy carrying a knife. Robert yes, Percy no. I can't see a motive for Ronald, other than Robert was just not very nice to him. Violet? I could see her having a motive to kill her husband to free herself to go to Robert, but not to kill Robert, unless, maybe she found out he was going to marry Maude? As I said earlier, Maude was having an affair with Robert and he had said he would marry her when they got back to England, but last night he had finished with her. So, both women might have motives.

Who can predict how another human will behave when their dreams are destroyed in front of them."

Major Fleming nodded. "What we have here are two love triangles. One is Maude, Violet and Robert. The other is Violet, Robert and Percy. Percy, I think could commit a violent murder and Percy could have faked taking his sleeping draught and waited for Violet to fall asleep, before going to Robert's room and murdering him. Maude had more opportunity, but Violet could also have sneaked out of the Osbourne's room after Percy took his sleeping draught. But who has the capacity to kill with a knife? I don't believe that of Maude or Violet."

Karolina decided to change the topic "James, can we also find out if Robert Smith was wealthy and when and where he got his money from?"

"That could be more difficult. If he was carrying a large amount of cash, then it wasn't in his luggage. That might have been the motive for the robbery. If he has it in a bank, we might be able to find out, but we would need to know first, which one of the many banks it might be in."

Alex also wanted to raise another potential lead. Ronald had provided an interesting piece of new information. "The investigation of the Italian authorities interests me. That might give us another lead on who could have killed Robert. Major, do you think you could go through channels to find out more about it?"

"Yes, Lieutenant, Let's not forget that. While your team is working on decrypting the radio communications, I'll telegram the authorities for more information."

"Good enough" replied Alex, "Karolina, are you going to be okay today if I go with Major Fleming to do some work for him?"

"Of course," replied Karolina. "You boys go and play with your secret inks and things. I think I'll take it easy today after last night's excitement. Maybe have a nap and catch up on my sleep."

The three of them rose and left the private room they had been using. They said their goodbyes in the lobby and Karolina watched them leave the hotel.

Chapter 12

Once James and Alex had left the lobby, Karolina turned to go to the reception desk. She was surprised to see Lady Felshaw and her son at the far side of the lobby. She appeared to be attempting to sneak by without Karolina spotting her. With a smile Karolina called out "Lady Felshaw! How good to see you again. I didn't realise we were all staying in the same hotel. How nice."

"Yes dear, very nice, however we must go. So nice to see you again," replied Lady Felshaw and quickly hurried past. Her son shrugged his shoulders and smiled at Karolina before turning away and trailing after his mother.

Karolina smiled to herself at Lady Felshaw's behaviour, but at least her son didn't seem upset with her. Perhaps there was hope for him yet. After her late night the night before she decided to find somewhere peaceful, where she could relax in the sunshine. She walked over to William on reception and said, "William, is there some place where I can get a little sun?"

"A little gun Miss! Whatever would you be wanting a gun for miss!"

"No William," said Karolina, raising her voice a little more and being sure to enunciate clearly. "I said, where can I get a little sun? Where can I sit in the sunshine!"

"Oh, right miss. You want to sit in the sunshine, you should have said so first. We have a nice terrace on the roof with views across the harbour. Plenty of sun for you there miss. Should have said that first rather than goin' on talking 'bout guns."

Murder on Malta

Karolina smiled, deciding there was no need to let William know that she was not in need of a little gun, because she already possessed a very effective Smith and Wesson 38, a present from her mother. "Thank you, William. The roof terrace sounds just the thing. Have a good day," and she walked off to the stairs rising from the far corner of the lobby. She didn't notice the guest with red hair, who had been reading his newspaper in the lobby, fold his newspaper up and tuck it under his arm, before following her to the stairs.

On the roof terrace, Karolina took a seat at one of the small tables. William had been right. From this height the views were fantastic looking out over the harbour and the city. A white jacketed waiter, in charge of the terrace, emerged from a small bar in the corner. He introduced himself as Mario, before asking if she would like something to eat or drink.

"I think I'll have a cappuccino, please, Mario" requested Karolina and she sat back to study the view.

She was watching the various ships in the harbour and admiring a particularly attractive steam yacht, when she was interrupted by a voice from her left.

Seated at the next table to her was a well-dressed red-haired man, wearing a business suit and holding a folded-up newspaper. "Very sorry to disturb you, but I couldn't help overhearing that wonderful accent when you spoke to the waiter. By any chance would you be the beautiful young American millionaire heiress that the staff are talking about?"

"Well, I'm American, but I'm not sure about the rest," she replied.

He laughed, "I apologise. I think the staff has a tendency to exaggerate and romanticise, but if it's not too forward, I don't think they were exaggerating when they described you as beautiful!"

"Thank you, sir. I don't think it can ever be too forward to complement a lady."

"My name is Walter Arrowsmith. Very pleased to meet you my dear."

"Karolina McAllister. Pleased to meet you also."

Just then, Mario arrived with Karolina's coffee and asked Walter if he would also like a drink. Walter declined and for a moment or two they both sat in silence studying the harbour.

"If it's not indelicate to ask, have you heard of the terrible murder that occurred last night?" Walter asked.

Karolina was a little surprised that the death was already publicly known to be a murder, but supposed that that sort of salacious gossip would spread quickly. Karolina replied to the question with a non-committal, "Yes, I have."

"I understand the gentleman's name was Robert Smith?"

"You seem to be exceptionally well informed, Mr. Arrowsmith?"

"Just listening to the staff talk," then perhaps feeling that more explanation was required said, "Actually I'm a newspaper reporter."

"Oh dear. I'll have to watch my 'p's and 'q's around you then," said Karolina with a smile.

"Oh, please don't worry, I'm not working now. Just naturally curious I'm afraid. I hope I haven't upset you? Were you close to the gentleman?"

Karolina was a little surprised that Walter hadn't picked up on her 'p's and 'q's joke but supposed he may have been tired of hearing it. "No, we weren't close. I'd only spoken to him a couple of times."

"A friend or a colleague perhaps?"

Karolina was beginning to feel a little uncomfortable with Mr. Arrowsmith's questions. "Neither in fact," she replied, declining to give any more information.

"I'm so sorry, Miss McAllister. My natural curiosity never knows when to shut up. I was just surprised when I saw it was the military police involved rather than the local police . . . " He paused, perhaps hoping Karolina would offer some comment, but when she didn't, he continued, "It must be terrible for the hotel. That sort of thing can damage their reputation. They must be very keen to know when the authorities will leave and they can get back to normal business . . . " again Mr. Arrowsmith left a pause and again Karolina failed to say anything. "Well, I'm very sorry to have bothered you, Miss McAllister. I'll let you get back to enjoying the sun and the view. I have some letters to write but I hope I'll see you again." Standing up he gave her a short bow and a smile, which she returned politely and left Karolina to her thoughts.

A little while later, when Mario came to take her empty cup, she asked him if he knew anything about Mr. Arrowsmith. "I'm afraid I don't miss. I don't think he's been here long. I think he checked in last night and this is the first time I've seen him."

Karolina stayed on the roof terrace for quite a while longer enjoying the sun and feeling quite sleepy. When she actually caught herself dozing off, she decided it was time to retire to her room. She thanked Mario and settled her bill, together with what she thought

Murder on Malta

was a modest tip. She was unaware that her generosity with the size of her tips, together with her unfamiliarity with the currency, were both factors in confirming her reputation amongst the staff as 'that American millionaire heiress'. Rising from the chair she made her way back down to the lobby, where she saw William behind the desk. Making sure to talk loudly and clearly, she approached William, "William, could you do me a big favour?"

"Course I will miss, what can I do for you?"

"There's a gentleman staying in the hotel, a Mr. Arrowsmith, I'm sure I know him from somewhere but I'm not sure where. What do you know about him?"

"Mr. Arrersmith, did yer say miss? Let me look up the register . . . Ah yes 'er he is. Walter Arrersmith. 'E wrote his home address as Limehouse, London. Checked in last night. Staying until tomorrow. Sorry miss, don't know nothin' more about him. Manager must have checked him in last night after I finished my shift. I can ask around if you like, miss?"

"Oh, don't go to any trouble. I'm sure I'll remember where I know him from eventually. Thank you for your help, William." Karolina thought she might just be overreacting to the man's simple curiosity and decided to dismiss Mr. Arrowsmith from her thoughts.

After a brief nap in her room Karolina decided to check on Maude. After knocking on the door to her room, Maude eventually answered and opened the door wide enough that Karolina could see she was teary and red eyed. "Come on Maude. Let me in and we will get you looking presentable and then you can come downstairs and keep me company over lunch."

"No. Really. I don't feel like eating anything."

"That's why you're just coming to save me from having to eat on my own," insisted Karolina.

Maude slowly and reluctantly opened the door and Karolina went in. "Let's start by washing your face, then we'll put on a little make up. If a girl looks good, then she'll feel better too!" Soon Maude was looking more presentable and ready to leave her room. Slipping Maude's arm through her own, she and Karolina closed the door behind them and made their way to the stairs. "I've found the hotel has a very nice roof terrace, where we can order a little food and sit in the sun," said Karolina and led Maude back to the terrace and the same table she had sat at earlier. When Mario the waiter came across, she studied the menu and ordered some tapas, together with some sparkling Italian white wine.

Within seconds, the waiter returned with an ice bucket and stand, a bottle of ice-cold white wine and two glasses. Making a show of opening the bottle and then wrapping a cloth around the neck of the bottle, the waiter poured each of the ladies a glass of wine. Bowing slightly to Karolina, he asked if there was anything else he could do for her before retiring to the bar, still keeping a careful eye on their table just in case they might need something more.

Karolina sipped her wine and asked Maude, "How are you feeling now dear?"

"Better, I suppose. It was all such a shock."

"I understand Maude. I lost my fiancé towards the end of the war and when we were told I was in shock for quite a while."

Maude looked Karolina in the eyes for the first time since she had left her room and then spontaneously reached across the table to squeeze her hand. "Then you know what it's like?"

Karolina nodded, though she thought that Maude had probably been lucky that Robert had not lived longer to hurt her even more. She doubted if Robert ever had any intention of marrying Maude once they were back in England. "My advice is that sitting in your room by yourself is not the best way to deal with it. You'll end up wallowing in self-pity. Find something to do, something to stop you thinking about it all the time."

Maude sniffed and nodded her head. "Thank you, Miss McAllister. It helps knowing I can talk to someone else who knows what it's like."

"Well, we can talk anytime, but you'd better start calling me Karolina instead of Miss McAllister if you want us to stay friends!"

Maude gave a brief smile then sipped her wine.

"I was thinking about Percy Osbourne earlier. He really didn't get on with Robert, did he?"

"Oh no Miss McA…. sorry, Karolina, they didn't get on very well at all. Robert said that Percy was stupid even if he did have a degree and also that he was not very good at his job. Robert said he could do a better job of it if he was only given half a chance."

"And do you think he could have done a better job."

Maude looked embarrassed for a second before saying, "We're not really supposed to talk about what we do Karolina, but what we do really is quite difficult. Very few people have the right sort of mind. I think that maybe Robert always felt like he could do things better than everyone else, but that people were holding him back because he didn't go to university, but I don't think that was true"

"Is Alex good at his job?"

"Oh yes miss. He's very good. He has an instinct for it. There might be three different ways to try to solve a problem and he always seems to guess which is going to be the best way to do it."

"Do you like Alex?"

"He's nice enough. He is always very kind to me and never gets annoyed with me. Robert did sometimes."

"What about Percy? Does he get annoyed with you? Does he have a temper?"

"Oh yes miss. I've seen him throw things off his desk when he can't solve a problem. And he shouts a lot when he doesn't get his way."

"I imagine Ronald isn't the sort to do that is he? And please don't call me miss. Remember it's Karolina."

Maude smiled and looked shyly down at the table, then looked up. "No, I've never seen Mr. Findlay get angry."

"Robert didn't seem to treat Ronald very respectfully, did he? Not like he was his superior?"

"No. Robert didn't think very much of Mr. Findlay at all. In fact, he told me some not very nice things about Mr. Findlay."

"Really Maude. What was that?"

"No. I can't repeat it Karolina. It was very rude."

Karoline looked at Maude. She obviously wanted to tell her what it was, but to her credit didn't want to be a gossip. "Maude, anything about Robert might help us to understand who could have done such a terrible thing to him. If you know anything that could help us,

Murder on Malta

you need to be strong and tell us. We'll keep it confidential as long as it doesn't stop us from catching Robert's murderer."

Maude looked shaken as she listened to the serious tone of Karolina's voice. After a few seconds she leant towards Karolina and said in a whisper, "Robert said that he had proof that Ronald was, . . . peculiar." Seeing Karolina's puzzled expression, she went on, "You know, " she struggled to find another way of saying what she wanted to say, "he was different . . . not like the other men." Still struggling for words, she said, ". . . didn't like girls. He'd had an affair with another man! Robert had the letters!" Finished with her revelation she sat back, blushing bright red.

Mario the waiter chose that moment to appear, with a tray loaded with tapas. Karolina recognised the pita bread, hummus, olives, capers, artichokes, and sundried tomatoes, but asked Mario what the other dishes were.

"This is biggilia miss. It is mashed black beans, and this very fine Maltese peppered cheese. The crackers are called galette. Very, very popular here." He proceeded to unload the tray, balancing it on one hand while removing each dish in turn, miraculously without the tray ever becoming imbalanced. Karolina was reminded of the music hall acts that ran around the stage with towers of cups and saucers precariously balanced, always on the point of falling. When he had finished this balancing act, he turned to Karolina and gave her a crisp bow and a wide smile. She wondered if the waiter now expected a round of applause, but all he wanted was to find out if there was anything else he could do. Finding there was nothing, he cheerfully went back behind the bar to await his next summons.

The arrival of the food had broken the flow of Karolina's careful questioning, so instead she smiled at Maude and insisted that she eat something from the delicious array of food. At first Maude declined, but it wasn't long before hunger overcame her as she nibbled away at the selection. As she ate, she asked Karolina, "You said your fiancé died in the war? Was he killed in the trenches?"

Karolina sighed and looked away. She remembered the sadness she'd felt at the time following Randolph's death. Even now, whenever that sadness returned, she had trained herself to think about the good memories instead. Memories when they had been childhood friends. "No, Maude. He didn't die in the trenches. He never made it that far. He caught 'flu on the troopship and was hospitalised when he arrived in France. I was told he didn't suffer and died within a few more days."

"I'm so sorry."

"Please don't be. He was a wonderful man and I'm glad that I knew him and that I have some wonderful memories."

"How did you meet him?"

"We had known each other since we were young children. He was a few years older than me, so of course I idolised him and followed him around. We grew up together and our parents just seemed to always assume we would get married." When Karolina thought about that, she always wondered how it would have worked out. The best memories of him were from their childhood, but as she'd grown into a woman, they had butted heads much more often, with him always sure he was right and never hesitating to tell her so. As she grew more confident and realised that she had a mind and opinions of her own, he had not liked that. When he had told her he had signed up 'to fight the Hun in France', getting engaged before he went had seemed the right thing to do. Now, she wondered how they would have got on as a married couple.

"Are you walking out with Alex now? I think he's very nice."

"Good God no!" replied Karolina. "I mean no, we're just, you know. . . We're just, well we're friends. Travelling companions!" she said, pleased to have found a description that didn't imply any degree of attraction between them, although Maude seemed surprised at the strength of her denial. After saying that they were just travelling companions, Karolina paused and thought about her relationship with Alex. He was very nice. He was always kind and considerate. And she knew he had a good sense of humour as well. Physically he had a great body. She thought momentarily of the statue of David she'd studied in Florence. Her mother would have said that Alex, 'scrubs up nicely doesn't he'. Suddenly Karolina realised Maude had asked her another question. "I'm sorry Maude, I was distracted by the . . . by the view! What did you say?"

"I said, When Alex, Percy and Ronald come back, I'm going to tell them that I feel much better now and will be able to work with them tomorrow. As you said, working will keep me occupied and stop me thinking about Robert. Talking to you has helped me a lot. Thank you so much Karolina."

"You're very welcome, Maude. Would you like to return the favour and keep me company when I go for a walk through the town? As a young woman, I feel a little nervous walking by myself in strange places." She was a little surprised that Maude seemed to accept such a blatant untruth, but was pleased when she said she'd be happy to accompany her. They finished of the meal and Karolina paid the bill, together with another generous tip for Mario, without realising that the size of the tip irrevocably confirmed her status in his eyes and subsequently in the eyes of the rest of the hotel staff as an American millionaire heiress.

Chapter 13

Alex returned from the military headquarters exhausted. The lack of sleep the previous night together with today's long hours of concentration had worn him out. Returning to his room, at first, he did nothing other than stand in front of his window, place his hands on his hips and stretch backwards, enjoying the feel as his muscles recovered from being hunched over a desk all day. Gradually his attention was drawn to the fantastic view from his window. Laid out in front of him was the panorama of the harbour, with ships and boats making their way in and out. Others were moored within the safety of the harbour. He saw that an old three-masted, squared rigged ship was newly arrived in harbour and that the beautiful white steam yacht, decked with flags and bunting was still there. Alex watched some of the crew of the steamship using a small davit and hoist to lower red fifty litre fuel drums one at a time into a small boat alongside. Alex supposed that the fuel would have been used to power an on-board electrical generator on the luxurious yacht and that the crew were now returning the empty drums to be refilled. As his eyes moved downward to the buildings below him, he saw the building with the roof top terrace. He now realised it was the roof of the nightclub he had visited the night before. The young lady with her hair tied back in a long pony tail, who had been rearranging her plants in the colourful blue or yellow plant pots, was still working on them today. He recognised her as the owner and singer from the night club. He watched her work with interest for several minutes, before stepping back from the window. He had promised himself a reward after his work today and now he decided it would be a good quality scotch whisky before dinner. Leaving his room, he was crossing the lobby on his way to the ground floor bar, when he met Karolina and Maude coming in from the street. The doorman held the door open for them as they entered, raised his hat and welcomed them with a bright "Good afternoon, Miss McAllister.

Alex waved when he saw them and crossed the lobby to greet them both, before asking Maude, "How are you feeling now Maude? Hopefully a little better?"

"Thank you, Alex. Yes, a little better. I feel I will be able to work tomorrow. Karolina has been wonderful." She smiled at Karolina, "She's keeping me distracted and not letting me dwell on things."

"We've been doing a little shopping in town this afternoon," Karolina said to Alex. Looking around the lobby she asked him, "Why do they have sheets covering the mirrors?"

"I think it's a tradition in some cultures. When someone dies, they cover the mirrors. I think the concern is that mirrors can trap the souls of the recently deceased on their journey to the afterlife."

Karolina noticed Maude's face fall at mention of Robert's death, and she turned to her. "Maude why don't you go up and rest before dinner, I have to talk to Alex for a few minutes."

Maude nodded and began to climb the stairs back to her room. Karolina watched her go then signalled Alex to follow her into the lounge. As she entered, Georgio greeted her with a cheerful, "Good afternoon, Miss McAllister! Can I get you a drink or something to eat?"

"No thanks. We're good," she replied.

"Actually, I'll have a large scotch whisky, thank you for asking," said Alex before the waiter could turn away.

Murder on Malta

"Oh, all right," said Karolina as Georgio turned back, "I'll have a bourbon on the rocks."

They took some seats by the window, where they had a good view of the street outside, where three karozzin carriages stood with no horses in their shafts. Two small boys were brushing the horses' coats down, while the horses drank from the water trough in front of the hotel and their owners sat at tables outside the coffee house next to the hotel.

"How was your hush-hush work today, Alex?"

"Not bad. It's actually proving easier than I expected, but I really shouldn't be talking to you about it."

"Don't worry. I won't tell anyone. You heard that Maude said she may feel well enough to help tomorrow."

"Yes. That's good. She will be a big help."

"While you've been at work decrypting secret messages, I've been hard at work too. It turns out the Ronald may have had a motive to have killed Robert after all."

"Really? What did you discover?" Alex leaned forward to better hear her reply.

Karolina lowered her voice, "It turns out that Robert had found out that, to use Maude's words, Ronald was 'peculiar'."

"Peculiar? Peculiar how?"

"He didn't like girls!" exclaimed Karolina triumphantly.

"Well, it's not exactly earth-shaking news," declared Alex. "There's a lot of men, even in high positions, that prefer the single life."

"But Robert told Maude it went further than that. That he'd had an affair with another man and Robert had their letters."

"Hmmmn. That's different. That is much more serious. If our masters in London had found out about that, it would have been the end of his career at the very least. It is still against the law in England, even though I'm sure it goes on all the time. As far as I'm concerned, if it's behind closed doors, it's no business of mine. The trouble is, Ronald's handling secret information continually as part of his job. Anything that lays him open to blackmail, would immediately get him sacked."

At that moment Georgio arrived with their drinks on a tray together with a jug of water and a bowl containing several ice cubes. After Georgio had served their drinks, he offered to pour water or put more ice cubes in Karolina's drink for her. She smiled and refused. He appeared disappointed but then hopefully offered to bring her some snacks or a meal, which Karolina again smilingly refused.

After he had gone, Alex remarked "Very attentive service in this hotel, isn't it?"

Karolina emitted a low growl. "I think that someone, maybe Lady Felshaw, has put it about that I'm an American millionaire heiress and now the staff are falling over themselves to do things for me." Alex had seen the size of some of the tips that Karolina had left and had a pretty good idea that they must have at least contributed to the rumour.

Alex smiled, "Seems a little ironic that you pretended your fiancé was a millionaire railway tycoon and your father was an oil millionaire in order to avoid Lady Felshaw's matchmaking attempts and now you're complaining about being treated like a millionairess!"

Alex quickly wiped the smile off his face as Karolina turned to glare at him. "Anyway," she said, "Do you think that maybe Robert was blackmailing Ronald?"

"That might explain where his sudden wealth came from, but blackmailers tend to keep asking for more payments over time. It seemed like Robert's wealth came in one big lump."

"Maybe Robert's wealth came from blackmailing someone else. Maybe this was the first time Robert tried to blackmail Ronald, and he responded by killing Robert?"

"I don't know. It's just difficult for me to see Ronald doing something like stabbing a man."

"I know. I think the same. And Maude said she had never seen Ronald lose his temper. But that's another thing. Did you know that Percy could get violent?"

"I hadn't seen it myself, but I knew he had difficulty with his temper. Robert especially used to like winding him up. He just never seemed to know when to stop."

At that moment, they both became aware of another guest standing close to their table. Karolina looked up and recognised the man who had approached her on the balcony earlier that day.

"Oh, hello. Mr. Arrowsmith isn't it, "said Karolina.

"Yes, Miss McAllister. Good to see you again. And is this gentleman your young man?"

"He's *not* my young man!" replied Karolina, clenching her teeth. "This is Alex Armstrong."

"I'm so sorry. I didn't mean to insinuate anything. I shouldn't have said anything. I just saw you both talking and wondered how you were doing?"

"We're fine Mr. Arrowsmith. Is there something we can help you with?" asked Karolina.

"No. No. . . . I was just noticing they still have guards on the room where that terrible business occurred. Seems like they're taking an awfully long time to sort it out, don't you think?

"I'm sorry Mr. Arrowsmith, we can't help you. Perhaps they're just being very thorough?"

"There's thorough and there's wasting time. How long do you think before they finish whatever it is they're doing and the hotel is back to normal, do you know?"

"As I said Mr. Arrowsmith, I'm afraid we can't help you. Maybe if you asked the hotel manager, he could reassure you?"

"Yes. Yes, It's no business of mine. It's just casual curiosity you know. Did you know the gentleman who died, Mr. Armstrong?"

"I did. We used to work together."

"Really?" Mr. Arrowsmith suddenly seemed to become more interested in Alex. "Were you friends?"

"I suppose you could say that. May I ask what's your interest Mr. Arrowsmith?"

"Oh, nothing really, just casual curiosity as I said. Well, I'll let you two carry on with you conversation. I expect I'll see you both around the hotel. Have a good day" So saying Mr. Arrowsmith left the lounge, but not before throwing one last glance over his shoulder at Alex.

Chapter 14

They sat at their table in the lounge window, watching Mr. Arrowsmith leave. "What did you think of that?" asked Karolina.

"I'm not sure. He could just be a nosey parker I suppose. Goodness knows there are enough of them about."

"But he seemed very focused on Robert's murder," pointed out Karolina. "He didn't seem to be interested in anything else."

"Agreed. Now that you mention it, it does seem suspicious. I think I'll ask Major Fleming to check Mr. Arrowsmith out."

"Good idea. Now, on a different topic, how would you feel about an early dinner, then an early night tonight. I need to catch up on my sleep after last night's excitement.

"Excellent idea," replied Alex. "Would you like to eat here, or go out to eat?"

"Let's eat here, I'm too tired to walk around town looking for somewhere to eat."

Karolina put a couple of banknotes on the table and together they stood. As they began to leave Georgio quickly came out from behind the bar. "Leaving Miss McAllister? You wouldn't like to stay and have another drink perhaps?"

"No thank you Georgio, we're just moving to the dining room."

"Of course, Miss McAllister. Anything you want. I could bring some drinks, perhaps an aperitif to your table, if you wish?"

"Alex, what about a white wine while we study the menu?" asked Karolina.

"Excellent idea."

"Certainly Miss McAllister. I'll bring it to your table right away"

Murder on Malta

As they walked away, Alex commented, "You know, there are definite advantages to dining with an American millionaire heiress!" then quickly ducked as Karolina tried to swat the back of his head.

On entering the dining room, they were personally shown to their table by the restaurant's maître d'hôtel, who took pleasure in explaining the various dishes on the menu. Eventually they both decided to start with aljotta which they discovered was a traditional and very garlicky Maltese fish soup. For a main course Karolina chose bragioli stew, which was slices of beef, pork and boiled eggs cooked in a sauce of tomatoes, carrots and peas. Alex decided on a local rabbit stew, again in a sauce of tomatoes, carrots and peas. They both declared their dinner to be excellent, before agreeing to go into the bar for a nightcap before an early night. As they entered the bar, Georgio looked up and his face broke into a smile. "Miss McAllister! Rocks with Bourbon on them, yes?"

Karolina nodded, capitulating to Georgio's enthusiasm to be of service and Alex asked for a scotch and water. Karolina whispered an aside to Alex, "Being an American millionaire heiress is getting to be very trying. The trouble is I'd hate to disappoint them by telling them I'm not. They seem to be enjoying it so much!"

"I think you're stuck with it now," smiled Alex. "Just try and accept it and enjoy being a celebrity."

As they approached the bar they saw, nursing a glass at the far end, the plump elderly gentleman with the bushy white moustache. Tonight, he was dressed in light coloured riding breeches, riding boots and what looked to Alex like a khaki safari jacket. Alex thought that at least it was an improvement over the kimono. As they approached, he hailed them, "Hello there, my young fella me lad! And I see you've brought your beautiful memsahib. Good to see yer both!"

"I'm *not* his memsahib!" replied Karolina forcefully, then turning back to Alex whispered "What's a memsahib anyway?"

Alex wondered how he could best translate memsahib to protect the colonel from Karolina's wrath. He whispered back to her "It's an Indian term of respect for a white female", then, more loudly he addressed the colonel, "Good evening, Lieutenant-Colonel Pinkersley. You're looking very well this evening!"

"Thank you, my boy! Very generous of you! I think I will" and he raised his glass to attract the waiter, before continuing, "Another large one here barkeep!"

"You're very welcome," laughed Alex, "This is Miss McAllister."

"Honoured to meet you miss!"

"Good to meet you as well colonel, although we did meet last night as well, you know."

"Did we by God! Well, I never! Must've clean slipped my mind. Don't normally forget a face, especially not one as pretty as yours! Are you sure?"

"Yes colonel. Quite sure. It was quite late though, so maybe it did slip your mind . . . "

"Really? Well, if you say so. I say, hope you don't mind me mentioning it, but do you know you have quite an odd accent!"

"Yes colonel. I'm American," said Karolina with a smile.

"Really? Are you certain? You would know I suppose. Yer know what, scuttlebutt in the mess here says there's another American gal around. Very beautiful apparently. Millionaire heiress don't you know. You should meet her!"

"We'll be sure to keep our eyes open for her colonel," said Alex with a smile, "we're taking our drinks into the lounge. Have a good night colonel!"

"Same to you, me young fellah. Take care of the little memsahib there! I'll keep my eyes on things here for a little while and maybe have one more snifter before lights out!"

Laughing, Alex and Karolina left the bar and went into the lounge to seat themselves at the same table as earlier that day. By now, night had fallen and lights had come on across the bay marking out where the land met the water. The water reflected the lights and the gentle movement of the waves made the reflection sparkle romantically. They sat in companionable silence for several minutes. Alex was the first to speak, "Are you missing home?"

Karolina didn't answer immediately. "I would have to say I'm missing my parents, but honestly, Texas, America? No, I don't think I am. It's so exciting to see new places and meet new and interesting people."

"Colonel Pinkersley for example?"

She laughed, "Yes, Colonel Pinkersley for example. I know you'll probably think it boring, but I'd love to sit down one night with the funny old bird and just let him tell us some of his stories. Just because he's old, doesn't mean his life story is boring. The opposite from what I've heard so far."

"You're right. When I got back from headquarters today, I was talking to William, the Hotel receptionist, you might think he had not much to tell, but the truth is the opposite. Did you know that after he was injured by the mortar in Gallipoli, he was put on a hospital ship and brought here with several hundred other casualties. And just one doctor on the ship? He bandaged himself up with the help of another soldier who had lost a leg. Got dressed and volunteered to help the nurses. Fell in love with one of them! When he arrived, they put him to work in one of the army hospitals and he eventually married his nurse. He was one of over fifty thousand casualties brought here from Gallipoli. Another fifty thousand came from the war in Salonica. Over one hundred thousand casualties were treated in Malta. One hundred thousand! It's no wonder they started calling Malta 'the Nurse of the Mediterranean'."

"I didn't know," said Karolina. She'd never even heard of the war in Salonica. She started wondering what her fiancé's experience had been in the hospital in France. She wondered if maybe he had fallen in love with one of his nurses as well. She knew it was supposed to happen all the time. She was surprised to find that she almost hoped he had fallen in love with his nurse as he lay dying in hospital. She wouldn't have begrudged him that one last happy experience. She looked at Alex sitting across the table, with a look of concern on his face and realised there were tears forming in her eyes. "Are you okay?" he said, "I'm sorry, did I say something wrong?"

"No, nothing wrong. Just a speck of dust in my eye. Would you like one last drink, then I really must get an early night, or I'll fall asleep at this table." She gave a small laugh and dabbed her eye with her handkerchief.

Alex knew there was no speck of dust, but he just didn't know what to say or do to fix whatever had upset her. Still worried, he decided to go along with her suggestion and signalled Georgio for two more drinks.

Chapter 15

After they had finished their drinks, they rose and Alex escorted Karolina through the lobby where she was intercepted by the hotel manager. Mr. Critchley greeted her and asked if she was sure that everything was to her satisfaction and that there was absolutely nothing more he could do to make her stay more pleasurable. Reassured he eventually let her and Alex take the stairs up to their rooms. After she had unlocked the door to her room and he had seen her safely across the threshold, Alex bade her good night and went to his adjacent room. Opening the door and switching the electric light on, he crossed his room and drew the curtains closed. He stood where he was for a few seconds, studying the room closely. On the desk, lay a letter to his older brother that he was in the process of writing. Page one was on top of page two. He was fairly sure that he had stopped writing the letter, with page two on top, with the pen on top of that, to prevent any stray draught blowing the pages around. The pen was now sitting neatly to the side of the letter. Without moving, he carefully looked around the room. He was certain his empty cases had been opened and moved. He also noticed several articles of clothing that seemed to have been moved as well.

Quickly leaving his room, he went to Karolina's door and knocked. Karolina came to the door after a few seconds, wearing a stunning long black silk nightgown.

"Why, Mr. Armstrong, I'm afraid I'm not dressed for receiving." Then, while looking at him through half-closed eyes she said in a sultry voice, "or perhaps that's what the gentleman intended?" and fluttered her eyelashes at him.

"What! No!" I didn't. I didn't think you'd have your nightgown on. No! I mean . . . "

Karolina stretched her arm upwards to lean provocatively against the doorframe, "Oh I think it's very obvious what you meant Mr. Armstrong. How very daring of you," and fluttered her eyelashes at him again.

"Damn it Karolina, I'm trying to be serious! Let me talk!"

"Well come in and talk then, I don't want to stand in the hallway in my nightgown chatting. Reaching out her hand she grabbed his arm and stepping aside, pulled him into the room. "So, what's so damn important at this time of night?"

"I just wanted to make sure you were okay."

"Why shouldn't I be?"

"When I got back to my room and looked around, I was pretty sure it had been entered and searched."

Karolina stared at Alex for a second. She'd come to trust him when he said something that she would dismiss as fanciful from other people. She was well aware of his keen observational senses. "I won't ask if you're sure, because you obviously are." She looked around her suite carefully. Nothing seemed out of place on the sofa or coffee table, nor the dining table and sideboard, except the drawers on the writing desk were not fully closed. She felt sure she had closed them. She moved into the bedroom, with Alex following her. Here again she carefully studied the bedside tables, chest of drawers and wardrobe. Had the mattress on the bed been moved and loosened the sheets? Opening the wardrobe and drawers, she checked her clothes. Then she went into the bathroom and studied her jewellery and makeup. Finally, she turned and looked up at Alex. "I can't be one hundred percent sure, but I think you're right. The jewellery I've worn was lying on top of the jewellery case. Now it's on the counter top. I think someone was looking inside the case.

Alex looked around the bathroom and the bedroom, then went back into the living room and checked the balcony. There wasn't anywhere he could see that was big enough to hide a man. "At least it looks like you're safe now. Will you be okay for tonight? Maybe prop a chair up against the door after I leave?"

Karolina nodded. Opening the drawer of one of her bedside tables, she removed her Smith and Wesson .38 revolver and checked that it was loaded, before replacing it. "I suspect that after they saw my little protector here, they'll think twice before coming back. Alex thank you for your concern. I really appreciate it, but I will be alright now." Alex turned and moved back towards the door and she followed him as he opened the door and as he turned and said goodnight, she stepped up and kissed him quickly on his cheek. "Good night, Sir Alex."

Chapter 16

Alex rose and dressed quickly the next morning. Once dressed, he stood at his window for a minute or two studying the view, thinking about last night. It was another fine sunny day and the waters in the harbour were glassily calm. Small boats were busily crossing the harbour. The locals were up and about in the streets below and the young lady with the pigtail was just leaving the roof terrace, after having arranged her blue and yellow plant pots to her satisfaction. Alex studied the view for a minute or two longer, then turned and left his room. Stopping at Karolina's room, her knocked on her door and waited. After a few seconds he nodded in silent approval as he heard a chair being dragged away from her side of the door before it was opened. Karolina stood there fully dressed, wearing her cream-coloured culottes, matching blouse and hip-length broad-belted blue jacket ready for the new day. She carried a small, handcrafted, brown leather bag with a long strap over her shoulder. She'd seen the bag for sale in Paris and thought it looked a little like an army officer's '*Musette*' bag. She had bought it, thinking it would be ideal for her, especially while doing archaeological field work.

"Disappointed that I'm not in my nightgown?"

"No, of course not. I mean . . . " Alex took a deep breath. She was always teasing him and trying to get him flustered. This time he was determined to stay calm and say something sensible. "You always look . . . wonderful. Whether you're wearing your nightgown or not." Horrified he suddenly realised the double meaning. He blushed bright red and struggled on. "I came to see if you'd slept okay and if you'd like to have breakfast."

Laughing Karolina said, "I would love to have breakfast with you and yes, I had an uninterrupted night's sleep last night."

Together they made their way down stairs into the lobby. As they were crossing the lobby, the hotel manager gave them a smiling greeting, "Good morning, Miss McAllister. I hope you had a good night's sleep. If there is anything, anything at all I can do for you please let me know."

Karolina came to a halt, midway across the lobby. Turning she approached the manager. "There is one thing you could do for me. From somewhere your staff have got the idea that I'm an American millionaire heiress. They really are making a big fuss over it. I would much rather just be treated the same as any other guest."

The manager looked at her, with a puzzled expression for a few seconds, then suddenly his face cleared and he broke into a smile. "Of course, Miss McAllister. I understand completely. Many of our guests prefer to travel incognito. I will have a discreet word with my staff." He gave her short bow, then turned away to go back behind the reception desk.

Karolina re-joined Alex and they resumed their progress towards the breakfast room. "Did you see that!", she said in exasperation. "He actually winked at me!"

All Alex could do was to try to supress his smile.

As they entered the breakfast room, they saw Major Fleming seated at a table in the corner, reading a paper. He looked like he had been waiting for them to appear, because as soon as they entered, he folded his newspaper, placed it next to his notebook on the table, then rose and greeted them.

"Lieutenant, Karolina, would you like to join me?"

"Thank you major," replied Karolina and she took the proffered chair next to him. James and Alex waited until she was seated, then seated themselves.

A smiling Georgio came immediately to Karolina's side and asked what she would like. "Chef has put eggs benedict on the menu especially for you, if you would like them?" She groaned in frustration, then ordered eggs benedict for her breakfast together with lots of strong black coffee. Alex and James also gave their order to the waiter and when he had left, James turned to Karolina and asked "Is there something the matter?

Karolina shook her head and said, "No. Nothing the matter. Just the service here is so . . . attentive. I don't even like eggs benedict!"

Alex jumped in, smiling, "The rumour's gone round that Karolina is a millionaire heiress and the staff can't do enough for her!"

James laughed. "That's right. William on reception, was telling me . . . "seeing Karolina glaring angrily at him, he rapidly changed direction, ". . . telling me that the weather should remain fine for at least another week."

Alex covered his mouth with the back of his hand and said in a fake whisper, "Good move. I don't think she noticed the switch of topic."

Karolina pursed her lips. "There are other tables I could move to you know."

James and Alex both laughed, before James said, "Please don't do that. I was hoping we could do a brief update on where we are and I'd appreciate both of your inputs."

Alex glanced quickly at Karolina, before saying, "Ronald and I are progressing well with . . . that work you gave us . . . and if Maude helps us, then I think we'll have it finished for you today."

"By 'that work' Alex means decrypting the secret messages from the foreign agents," said Karolina, feeling a little bit smug that she knew what was going on.

"Thank you, Karolina. Remind me to keep our other secrets well away from you."

"It's not me you have to worry about, it was Violet who blew the gaff and you who first mentioned foreign agents. Anyway, what are these other secrets?"

James pointedly ignored her question. "Well to continue with business, I've been in contact with the Italian authorities about the investigation that Robert was involved with. It appears that in the last year of the war, while we and the Italians were still fighting the Austrians, the Austrian cryptographic service got hold of three vitally important Italian code books, either through espionage, theft, or by bribery of someone with access to them. Robert's role involved travelling to various Italian radio stations, one of which was suspected to be the origin of the leak. There was no evidence against anyone specifically at the time and the Italians put it down to an opportunistic theft. In hindsight, Robert's sudden suspicious increase in wealth at around the same time was very interesting to the Italians."

"I hate to speak ill of the dead," said Alex, "but from what I knew of Robert's character, it wouldn't surprise me to find out he saw an opportunity to get rich and took it."

They put their conversation on hold, as Georgio placed their orders in front of them and after asking if they would like anything else, left them to their breakfasts.

Karolina took a sip of her coffee. "We've not made any real progress here, but there are some things I wanted to mention. We've found out that Maude was infatuated with Robert and he had led her to believe they would marry when they got back to England. After dinner last night, Maude caught up with Robert when he stopped at reception and he basically broke it off with her. That gives her a motive to kill him. Someone else with a motive is Ronald. Robert had something on him, that, if he hadn't actually used it to blackmail Ronald yet, he may have intended to do so. We also know Percy has a motive. He was bound to be jealous of the way Robert was flirting with his wife and it looked like the flirting was about to metamorphose into a full-blown affair. So that makes Violet about the only person without a motive."

Major Fleming had been writing rapidly in his notebook, trying to keep up with Karolina. When she finished and paused, he stopped and looked up at her. "This is what you call 'not much progress'?" he asked. "I need to watch your interrogation techniques. I might learn something from them. Do you prefer the old-fashioned Chinese water torture or the thumbscrews?"

"Typical man! You think you have to solve everything using force. I just sit and listen. People seem to want to talk to me."

Murder on Malta

"You say that Robert had something to blackmail Ronald with. Do you know what that was?"

"I'm afraid I can't say at the moment. I may be able to tell you later." Karolina felt a little guilty about misleading James with her choice of words, but felt she could always tell him the full story if needed later. "Anyway, there is one more thing. There is a Mr. Arrowsmith who is a guest in the hotel. He appeared to make a point of questioning me about the murder. He says that he is a newspaper reporter, which gives him an excuse I suppose, but he seems interested to know how long the military police will be here. What really worries me, is that last night he approached Alex and me and became very interested in Alex when Alex mentioned he was Robert's colleague and friend. Then, when we retired for the night, we found that our rooms had been searched. I may be putting two and two together and getting six, but it makes me wonder. Oh, and yes, one more thing, when he told me he was a reporter, I said I must mind my 'p's and 'q's and he didn't get my little joke.

Alex and James both looked at her with a puzzled expression on their faces. "Little joke?" asked James.

It was Karolina's turn to look puzzled. "Yes. 'p's and 'q's. It's an in-joke with printers. Because when they're setting up the individual letters, everything is reversed. So 'p's look like 'q's and vice versa. So, they have to take extra special care with them. That's where the saying comes from. I can't believe you didn't know that. Anyone in the print industry would." Karolina looked simultaneously disappointed that they hadn't got her joke and pleased that she'd known something that neither of them had.

Neither of the men said anything, until finally James said, "Well, it's something worth checking up on. I'll get his home address from the hotel register and telegraph his local police to see what they know about him. What was his name?"

"No, it wasn't Mr. Watt, it was Mr. Arrowsmith," said Karolina, pleased to have gotten another joke in."

James rolled his eyes. "Alright, Mr. Arrowsmith then. I'll get back to you on that, but for now, I think the lieutenant and I need to get back to work."

They all looked up as the major's sergeant marched briskly into the breakfast room and came up to the major. "The carpenter's been sir and fixed the door to Mr. Smith's room sir. I've locked the door and have the key."

"Major, would you mind me taking another look at that room, sir?" asked Alex. "I only gave it the briefest of inspections and there may be some detail that I missed."

"The sergeant and I have already thoroughly searched that room lieutenant," said the major before pausing and considering for a moment. "On the other hand, you have already proved to me that you have exceptional observational skills. I have no problem with you searching that room again, but for now I'd like you to prioritise the decryption work. Once we have some progress on that I have no objection to you doing whatever you want. Sergeant, give the key to the lieutenant in case I'm not around." He looked regretfully at his half-finished breakfast, before rising. "I'll get a landau and meet you outside in a few minutes. Sergeant, with me," he ordered, before rising from the table to leave.

Alex hastily pushed the last bite of his breakfast into his mouth and also got up. "I'll be there in a minute. What are you going to be doing today, Karolina?"

"I thought I'd have a word with a few of the staff and see if they saw anything of interest on that night."

"Sounds like a good idea to me, but please be careful. Whoever we are looking for is dangerous."

"So am I Alex!" And she tapped her small Musette bag hanging on the back of her chair. "I've decided that me and my special friends, Mr. Smith and Mr. Wesson will stick close together wherever I go until we catch the murderer."

"I'm not sure if that reassures me or not," he replied with a wry grin. "Just be as safe as you can."

Karolina smiled at him and Alex, leaning heavily on his walking stick, limped out of the breakfast room to find Major Fleming. She remained at the breakfast table enjoying the solitude while watching the other guests, until she noticed Ronald Findlay enter the breakfast room. She waved a hand to attract his attention and pointed to the recently vacated chair next to her.

"Good morning, dear thing! How are you today?"

"I'm very well Ronald. Please sit down and join me if you'd like?"

"I would like nothing better dear lady. What a wonderful way to start the day, breakfast with a young lady whose beauty exceeds that of the sun rising over the Mediterranean Sea!"

Karolina laughed. "Flattery always was the way to a lady's heart."

The waiter approached and took Ronald's order for breakfast. When he had departed, Karolina leaned in closer to Ronald and said quietly, "I'm afraid I have something very personal that I need to discuss with you Ronald."

"Really. That sounds very exciting dear lady. How can I help?"

"It's rather something that I need to warn you about, Ronald. As you know, Major Fleming is continuing to investigate into Robert's murder. Some information regarding your private life has come into my possession, that I have not shared with Major Fleming. It gives you a very strong motive to get rid of Robert. At the moment I see no reason to share details of your private life with Major Fleming, if you can re-assure me that you had nothing to do with Robert's murder."

Ronald's face had gone chalky white. His hands, resting on the tablecloth, started to tremble. It took him several seconds to pull himself together, before he could ask in a trembling voice, "Whatever can it be that you have found out?"

"Robert was in possession of certain documents concerning your relationship of an intimate nature with another .. shall we just say, another person?"

Ronald face fell. "Please, please dear lady, if you have those letters, I beg you to return them to me!"

"They are not in my possession at the moment, but they may come in to my possession in the near future. If they do, I cannot return them to you unless I can be absolutely certain of two things. One, that you had nothing whatsoever to do with Robert's murder and two, with this in your background, you cannot continue work with secret information. You are too open to blackmail. You must resign from your role, when you return to England."

"I will do anything you ask dear lady. I had already made up my mind to resign when I get back to England. Now the war is over, I want nothing more than a quiet retirement to my house in the country. I don't know how I can possibly prove I had nothing to do with poor Robert's death, but I will absolutely swear I did not. Tell me what I can do dear lady to prove it to you and I will do it!" pleaded Ronald.

Karolina had been carefully watching Ronald's face and expression as he had been speaking. Her instinct told her that Ronald was speaking the truth.

"At least for the moment Ronald, I am prepared to believe you, but you must tell me everything you know that might relate to Robert's murder. And think very carefully, because if I later find you held something back, I won't hesitate to share my information with Major Fleming! Was Robert blackmailing you?"

"No. At least not for money. Just for little things, like not working when he didn't want to. He would be as rude to me as he wanted and I couldn't say anything. I couldn't ever tell him what to do. He would just hint about the letters and I would have to give in."

"What do you know about his murder?"

Ronald looked panicked, as he desperately tried to recall anything that might be useful to Karolina. "I know nothing. I had nothing to do with it."

"I'm not asking if you did it. I want to know anything you heard, anything you saw that might tell us why he was murdered or who murdered him. Any little detail that might be relevant."

"My dear, I don't know anything of importance!" He paused for a second, perhaps trying to remember the night of the murder. "The only very minor detail I can recall that might be any help to you at all, is that after dinner that night, after Robert had said he was leaving to go to the casino, when I left you all to retire to my room, I did notice Robert was still at the reception desk, talking to the manager. Maude was there also. She seemed upset with Robert, I cannot recall anything else that might help you, but I promise you that if I do, I will tell you straight away."

It was only a small piece of information, but it re-enforced her plan to talk to the staff, to see what they might know about the suspects' movements on that fateful night. Karolina rose from her seat and looked directly into Ronald's eyes. "Very well Ronald, for the moment I believe you, but I warn you again, if you remember anything, or you discover something new, you need to let me know immediately. I will have no hesitation in revealing your secret to the authorities if you fail to co-operate fully."

"Oh, I will dear lady. I will. Thank you so much for being so compassionate and understanding. I am completely in your debt. Thank you again."

Karolina nodded and turned to leave the breakfast room. As she approached the door, she noticed the waiter had positioned himself next to it and was smiling at her. As she came closer, he opened the door for her and said, "Good morning, Miss McAllister, I hope breakfast was to your satisfaction?"

Resignedly Karolina said it had been wonderful and wished him a good day. When was she ever going to convince the staff that she was not a millionaire!

Once out in the lobby, she saw William on reception and Mr. Critchley the manager standing close by with his arms behind his back, smiling and nodding at the guests. As soon as he saw her, his smile became broader. He barely managed to stop himself from bowing to Karolina. He straightened his face and deliberately gave her the smallest of nods. "I swear he just winked at me again!" muttered Karolina under her breath. "Mr. Critchley. I wonder if I could have a quiet word with you?"

"Of course, Miss McAllister! It would be my absolute pleasure!"

"Mr. Critchley, I believe you are aware that Lieutenant Armstrong and I are working with Major Fleming in order to get the unfortunate incident with Mr. Smith cleared up as quickly and discreetly as possible?"

"I was not aware, Miss McAllister, but I'm quite sure the affair could not be in better hands. Anything, anything at all that I or my staff can do to help you resolve this terrible business, as you say, as quickly and discreetly as possible, then you only have to make the merest suggestion and we will comply with dispatch!"

"I quite understand Mr. Critchley and as it happens there may be something you can help with. On the night of the . . . unfortunate incident, did you see Mr. Smith at all, after dinner?"

"Yes Miss McAllister, I did!" said the manager enthusiastically. "Perhaps it would be more appropriate to continue our discussion in my office?" Mr. Critchley led Karolina into his office behind the reception desk. It was quite small, with no external windows, just a small wooden hatch in the wall behind the reception desk. Filing cabinets and cupboards covered the other three walls. The one concession to luxury was an extremely pretty tea set on top of one cupboard, together with a small kettle and paraffin stove. Once Karolina had taken the only seat in front of the desk, Mr. Critchley indicated the tea set and asked Karolina if she would like a cup. "It's the finest Earl Grey," he said with pride. When she politely refused, he nodded and took the seat behind the desk.

"You indicated that you might remember seeing Mr. Smith on the night of the unfortunate incident, Mr. Critchley?"

"I did. I happened to be behind the reception desk, when he came from the dining room. Of course, I don't usually work behind reception. I have staff to do that sort of work, but just at that moment, I happened to be standing there when he approached."

"He didn't just walk past? He came up to the desk for something?"

"Assuredly so Miss McAllister. As I remember it, he checked for his messages and then Miss Cooper came up to him. Then they began to argue about something. I am not sure of what was said, or what it was about, but Miss Cooper left in tears."

To Karolina, this seemed to tie in with the argument that Maude had told her about, where Robert, that rat, had dumped the poor girl. "Please do go on Mr. Critchley. Did Mr. Smith then go to his room?"

"No Miss McAllister. He asked for an envelope and notepaper. We have very high-quality notepaper here; I expect you will have noticed Miss McAllister?"

"Yes, Mr. Critchley I have, but please do go on. Did you happen to see what he was writing?"

"Oh no Miss McAllister! It would never do for myself or a member of staff to watch a guest when they were writing a private message!"

"So, you don't know who the message was for?"

Murder on Malta

"Oh yes Miss McAllister. Mr. Smith clearly wrote Mrs. Osborne's name on the envelope and asked for it to be given to her when she next passed through the lobby. I was given to understand from Mr. Smith that he thought she would be passing by very shortly. I believe he then went up to his room."

"Interesting. It's a pity we don't know what that note said. It could be crucially important."

"But we do know what it said Miss McAllister. I presented the note to Mrs. Osborne when she came through the lobby a few minutes later, following her husband. She read it there and then. When she had read it, she crumpled it up and tossed it on the reception desk."

"Where you read this private message?"

Mr. Critchley looked a little affronted. "Well considering the way she had discarded it; I took the view that this was no longer a private message."

"Please. If you could Mr. Critchley. Can you just tell me what it said?" Karolina's patience was rapidly wearing out and she was beginning to believe the man was deliberately trying to see how long he could draw out the conversation.

"I believe it instructed Mrs. Osbourne to come to Mr. Smith's room as soon as her husband was asleep!" If Mr. Critchley had shown a little disapproval at the thought of reading a guest's private correspondence earlier, he now looked completely affronted. In fact, Karolina felt that Mr. Critchley could probably give lessons to Queen Victoria on how not to be amused. He continued, "This is absolutely not the sort of activity we expect our guests to indulge in! There are of course other hotels where that sort of thing is tolerated, but ours is not one of them!"

At Mr. Critchley's use of the royal 'we', the comparison of Mr. Critchley to Queen Victoria, sprang unbidden into Karolina's mind again and caused her to struggle to suppress a smirk. When Mr. Critchley finished with, "We are not pleased!" she had to cover up her laughter with a hurried bout of fake coughing which then unfortunately turned into a bout of real coughing.

She waved away Mr. Critchley's concern and apologised, "Thank you Mr. Critchley. You really have been most helpful. I am sure Major Fleming will appreciate this valuable information and will want to convey his thanks to you personally."

Mr. Critchley smiled and looked very pleased with himself, but his expression suddenly changed to concern. "You will be very discreet with this information won't you Miss McAllister? It would not do if Mr. Smith and Mrs. Osbourne's behaviour became public knowledge. Not do at all. The reputation of the hotel is paramount!"

"I assure you that Major Fleming and I will be absolutely discreet and treat this information as confidential. Thank you again, Mr. Critchley and now, I have some other urgent business to check on. If you'll excuse me, Mr. Critchley."

As Karolina left the office, she stopped at the reception desk to ask if William knew where Violet might be.

"Yes, miss," replied William, "she's just gone shopping she has. Wanted to know if there were a 'boo-teek' in Valletta she said."

Karolina noted with interest that Violet appeared to have recovered from her grief quite quickly. She thanked William before asking William if he knew where Miss Cooper or Mr. Osborne could be found.

"Sorry miss. They've left as well. Left with the dashing young major a few minutes ago."

"Well William, it looks like I have the hotel to myself. If Mrs. Osbourne returns, can you please let her know I'm looking for her. In the meantime, I think I'll get my book and read it on that wonderful sunny roof terrace you told me about." She turned away from reception and ascended the stairs to go to her room. She failed to notice the guest with the red hair, standing behind a large aspidistra, who had been carefully watching her activities.

Chapter 17

When Karolina arrived on the terrace, she was pleased to see Lily sitting at one of the tables Her small white dogs were sitting obediently at her feet. Karolina approached her table and greeted her.

"Hello Lily! I'm so pleased to see you again! Would you mind if I joined you?"

"Not at all my dear girl," replied Lily. "Perhaps you'd like a cup of tea?"

Mario the waiter had already appeared and was hovering behind Karolina's right shoulder.

Turning to face him, Karolina said "I'd rather have a strong cup of coffee, Mario, if you please."

"Of course Miss Armstrong," replied Mario and left to arrange it.

Karolina turned back to Lily and said, "Your dogs are very well behaved. They look familiar, but I'm afraid I can't place the breed?" Both dogs were small, with silky, pure-white coats, soft drooping ears and fluffy tails that curved up over their backs.

The elderly lady looked down at her two dogs fondly and sensing their mistress's attention they both looked up at her at the same time. "They're Maltese Lion Dogs," she replied. "A very old breed and quite, quite, lovable. Getting old like me now, but I wouldn't be without them."

"I knew they were familiar! Did you know that one of Aesop's fables was about a Maltese Lion Dog. I'm an archaeologist and I have a passion for the history of Egypt. I believe I'm correct in saying that they were highly valued by the ancient Egyptians. They are shown in hieroglyphics as companions to the ladies of the Pharoh's harem. Egyptians also believed them to have the power of healing. They would have a Lion Dog in their bedrooms at night, with the belief that it would restore their health as they slept."

The old woman smiled at Karolina, "If you promise not to tell anyone, I have to admit that these two sleep on my bed with me too and I think I'm pretty healthy for my age. Now if you'll excuse me my dear, I need to take my two little angels for a walk. It's been so nice to see you again."

"Actually, I was thinking of going for a walk myself." Karolina hadn't been planning a walk at all, but she was enjoying the older woman's company. "Would you mind terribly if I came with you?"

"Of course not my dear. I'd be delighted. I was planning to go to the Lower Barrakka Gardens, if that's acceptable to you?"

"Absolutely – I have no idea where that is, but it sounds like fun! I take it you know Valletta well?"

"Yes my dear. I live an hour or so away in Mellieha Bay, but I treat myself to staying here every few weeks when I have errands to do, or when I've been travelling off the island."

Together the two women descended to the lobby and left the hotel. They walked a short distance, retracing Karolina's trip to the cathedral. As they walked, they pointed out to each other items of interest in the small shops lining both sides of the street. When they stopped to admire some lace in one window, Lily asked Karolina, "I saw you in the lobby yesterday, with a young man. Was he what you youngsters are now calling your boyfriend?"

"Oh no!" Karolina exclaimed. "We're travelling together and he's easy to get along with, or at least I can put up with him most of the time, but we're not involved with each other. No. He's lovely and he's a really good guy, but he's absolutely not my boyfriend. Of course, he does look very nice as well," she added almost as an afterthought.

Lily studied Karolina very thoughtfully for a minute before she continued, "Yes he is quite handsome, but of course most men look handsome in a uniform."

Karolina looked at Lily in puzzlement for a split second, then light dawned, "Oh, you meant Major Fleming! No, he's not my boyfriend either."

Lily gave Karolina one last thoughtful glance, but then, by mutual agreement they started to wander on down the street, stopping to examine the goods for sale in other shops.

"I find that interesting Karolina. The first young gentleman, the one you denied so strongly having any feelings for, what is your relationship with him?"

Karolina's first instinct was to tell Lily, not so politely, that her relationship with Alex was nothing to do with Lily and for Lily to mind her own business, but as she considered that, she reluctantly realised that making such a strong response would in a way confirm what Lily was implying. Why did she want to deny so strongly that there was any relationship between her and Alex.

Without really knowing why, Karolina blurted out "I was engaged to another man until recently."

Lily took the sudden change of topic in her stride. "Was?"

"Yes, was." Why was she now telling Lily about Randolph? He had nothing to do with Alex, did he? But for some reason she felt the need to tell Lily about her deceased fiancé. "We'd known each other since we were children. After he told me he'd signed up to fight in France, we became engaged, but he died of influenza before he could reach the front."

"I'm so sorry my dear. I can only imagine how you must feel."

Karolina stopped in front of another shop, but without actually seeing the items displayed. She continued to stare blankly in the shop window for several seconds. Lily stood by patiently, not hurrying her. Karolina was struggling to understand exactly how she did feel. She was surprised to find emotion welling up inside her.

She'd been asked about Randolph many times during her travels in Europe. In the past she'd always responded unemotionally and in a matter-of-fact way to the questions. Now, for some reason, talking to this kindly, elderly woman who listened so patiently, thoughtfully without interruption, it was very different. It was releasing feelings she didn't understand, or could even clearly identify. Feelings she did not remember having before. Was she grieving? Was she feeling loss? Was she regretting the loss of their future life together? Was she angry? Was she guilty?

Guilt? Where had guilt come from? She had no reason to feel guilty about Randolph. She had nothing to do with his death. She hadn't even wanted him to join up. She'd been furious when he told her that he had signed up without even discussing it with her beforehand. He had just laughed and ignored her. No, she said to herself firmly. She had no reason to feel guilty about Randolph's death. But then why could she not convince herself of that?

"I said, are you feeling alright dear?" Lily's voice penetrated her thoughts. "You look a little upset my dear. I do hope it's nothing I've said? The gardens are just a little way down this side street. The dogs are quite eager to get there. Perhaps we can sit on a bench and watch them play?"

Karolina was surprised. She had completely forgotten they were taking the dogs for a walk.

Nodding, but without saying anything more, she walked with a concerned Lily to the gardens and together they sat in silence on a bench in the sunshine and watched the two dogs running and chasing each other over the grass.

After several minutes, Lily reached out and squeezed Karolina's hand for a few seconds, then seemed content to sit in silence again and let Karolina continue to explore her own thoughts.

Eventually Karolina spoke. "I think you're a very wise woman Lily. You have a way of just sitting there in silence that feels very reassuring." Something she realised in surprise, that Alex could do as well.

"With age comes wisdom, they say" said Lily, with a gentle smile "but often it seems we act more and more like children as we get older. Would you like to talk about it now my dear?"

Karolina paused for several seconds considering if she wanted to discuss her feelings with this older woman. She surprised herself when she blurted out, "Why do you think I would feel guilty about my ex-fiancé?"

"When war takes someone close to us, people often feel guilty that they have survived. Or, we sometimes feel disloyal because we go on to find happiness that they'll never know."

When Lily mentioned happiness a picture of Alex sprang into her mind, with memories of their relaxed banter and growing friendship. But that was silly! She wasn't doing anything with Alex she should feel guilty about. Was she? Okay, she liked him. She enjoyed being with him. But she wasn't doing anything with him that would cause Randolph to be jealous. And she knew that Randolph could be jealous. Very jealous. This was silly, she was thinking like Randolph was still alive and that she was still engaged to him! The realisation disturbed her. She needed to think some more about this, but not now. Right now, she was being most impolite to her new friend. She didn't want to think this through now. She needed to be happy and entertaining. The two dogs were still racing around in front of them, with their tongues lolling out of their mouths as if they were laughing at some huge joke, occasional running back to their mistress and looking up at her face to make sure she was happy too.

"Lily, would you mind if we didn't talk about my fiancé now? Maybe we could just sit here in the sun, enjoying the dogs before we go back to the hotel?"

"I think that would be an excellent idea. I've always thought that watching dogs was both entertaining and educational. They always seem to simply appreciate the here and now and be much happier for it. Perhaps dogs are the really wise ones and us humans have a lot to learn from them."

Chapter 18

Karolina spent the rest of the afternoon quietly. She caught up with her letter to home and left it with William to post. Then she went and sat in the sun on the roof terrace, reading her book, in between closing her eyes and half-dozing. At one point she was awakened by a massive boom! When she sat up quickly looking concerned, Mario the waiter came over and explained it was only the naval time cannon being fired from the saluting battery close by. He made sure she didn't require any cold drinks, coffee or snacks before returning to his bar.

Around about lunchtime, she was getting bored and was starting to think about going for another walk, or finding out from William where she might go for a swim, when Alex came out onto the terrace.

She greeted Alex with "Good, I was getting bored. Now you can entertain me."

"I'm not sure of my entertainment value, but I do have news."

"Oh winged mercury, tell me more! . . . but first take a seat. Mario the waiter is dying to be useful. Would you like to order something to eat or a drink?"

As Karolina had expected, as soon as he had seen Alex arrive, Mario had jumped from his post behind the bar and was now standing expectantly, notepad in hand, behind Alex. Together they decided to order some white wine and Mario, now with a satisfactory mission to perform, departed to arrange it.

"Well, the first big news is that we've decoded the radio transmissions. We saw at once they weren't using military level encryption like the main protagonists had during the war. We suspected they were using a simple substitution cypher, with some added twist so that frequency analysis wouldn't work." Karolina nodded knowledgably. She could see Alex was excited and pleased with himself and she enjoyed seeing him this animated. She encouraged him to continue. "Well, we guessed that maybe the starting character for the substitution pattern changed every so often within the message and then it was just tedious boring work to try different frequencies of change and substitution patterns. Didn't take us long to hit on the correct combination, then we were able to read all the reports!"

"Don't drag it out! So, what did they say?"

"Mostly it was back and forth between the agent here and we guess the fascist's backers in Italy. The operative here asking for more money and the fascists telling him he had to make do. Even so, seems like a lot of money was funding the operation. Also, there were requests for propaganda posters and leaflets to be sent from Italy. Major Fleming wasn't surprised at that. He'd always thought it would involve too many people and be too risky to print that sort of material over here. Probably the most interesting thing was confirmation that the operation is based here in Valletta and the operative here works under the code name of 'Sparrow'."

Mario arrived at this point with glasses and a bottle of cold white wine, which he proceeded to pour for them. As soon as Mario had departed, Alex continued, "Another thing, remember you asked Major Fleming if he could check up on that guest Mr. Arrowsmith? Well, he was quite pleased with the results. The telegram came back from Limehouse Police in London. Your newspaper reporter is no newspaper reporter! He is well known to the police. He's a convicted fence, that's slang for a seller of stolen goods, and he's suspected to be the leader of a gang of jewel thieves. He is also suspected of being responsible for the murder of one of his gang members. Probably a falling out over the division of the spoils. But what really got the major excited was how the man died. Stabbed with a long, narrow-bladed knife!"

"I knew it. Is the major going to arrest him."

"First, he wants to find more evidence, before taking him in for questioning, but he's at the top of the major's suspect list now. He wanted me to tell you, under no circumstances must you try to approach him or talk to him. The police think he's a very nasty character. I know you're a very capable young lady and can handle most things, but please, take care of yourself. We can solve this without taking any unnecessary risks. The major wants you to stay out of trouble!"

"I'm not sure why the major thinks I would get myself into trouble!"

"Really Karolina? You don't know why anyone would think that you could get into trouble?" Alex continued quietly but insistently, "Look, I respect your independence and admire your confidence and capabilities, but please, please, don't take risks that are unnecessary!"

Grudgingly Karolina agreed with Alex, "Ok. I promise I will avoid any unnecessary risk, but only if you do me a favour in return."

"And that would be . . . ?"

"I spoke to Ronald. He admitted that Robert was in a position to blackmail him with those letters about his love life, but that he hadn't actually asked for money. He just held them over his head and made Ronald do anything he wanted."

"Do you believe him?"

"I do. Robert may have been planning to extort money from Ronald at some time in the future, perhaps if his own money ran out, but he hadn't yet descended to that."

"You believe Ronald is innocent them"

"Yes, I do. He was absolutely terrified. He was too frightened to lie to me. He thought I had the letters and I was going to turn him in. He swore that if I would promise to destroy those letters, he would resign his job immediately on his return to England. I told him that I would do the best I could to prevent the letters falling into the hands of the authorities, but if I found out he had lied, or not told me everything, I would have no hesitation in handing them over."

Karolina paused and took a sip of her drink. "He did tell me one thing of interest. After he left us that night and was on his way to his room, he saw Robert at the reception desk talking to Mr. Critchley. I tracked down Mr. Critchley and asked him what Robert had said. Mr. Critchley said that after Robert picked up his own messages, that rat left a message for Violet, asking her to come to his room later that night!"

"That's fantastic work Karolina! And did she go to his room?"

"That's what I'm waiting to find out. And speak of the devil, here comes Violet now. Quickly, before she arrives. You have the key to Robert's room. You said you were going to search it. If you find those letters, will you hang on to them?"

Alex hesitated in replying to her. "Please Alex. I'm sure he's innocent and telling the truth. At least hold onto them for a short while. Please!" Before she could get an answer, Violet arrived at their table.

"Good afternoon, Karolina. Alex." She nodded and smiled knowingly at each of them. "I do hope I'm not interrupting anything," although it was obvious from her expression that she assumed she was in fact interrupting something. "That old man at reception told me that you wanted to see me?"

"Good afternoon, Violet. I do indeed. Would you like to take a drink, maybe share a cocktail with me? Alex was just about to leave."

"Oh yes," replied Violet. "Can we have another one of those Manhattan's. That was lovely!"

"Yes, of course we can." She signalled Mario and ordered the drinks. ". . . and Alex, if you are going to do that job now, you will think about what I've just said?"

Alex picked up his walking stick and used it to help him rise from his seat. "I'll think about it, however there are rules that have to be followed with such things. I'll see you for dinner this evening Karolina. Good day Violet." And Alex limped from the balcony.

"Alex doesn't seem too happy, Karolina?"

"Oh it's nothing. I just want him to take some time off from his work and show me Valletta, but he says he has to work. That's all."

Violet looked over her shoulder, following Alex's departure and seemingly unconvinced with Karolina's story.

Karolina wanted Violet to stop thinking about Alex and fortunately Mario distracted her when he arrived with their cocktails. Once he had left, Karolina said, "Violet, you know that Major Fleming and I are investigating Robert's death." Karolina waited, to make sure she had Violet's full attention. She seemed more interested in watching the waiter's retreating figure. "You know it's very important that you tell us anything that might help us?" She waited for Violet to look at her and nod. "If you don't tell us everything, or worse, if you lie about something, you could be in very serious trouble with the authorities."

"I haven't lied about anything Karolina! I've always told you the truth!"

"Think very carefully now Violet before you answer this. Did you get a message from Robert on the night he was murdered?"

Karolina could see that Violet was thinking very carefully before answering. Whether it was to see what she could get away with in her answer, or to make sure she told the whole truth was the question."

"I did. It was just to see if Percy and I could meet him for breakfast."

"Violet. We know you received a message from him and we know what it said. Do you want to try again? I'm giving you one last chance!"

Violet looked at Karolina and still seemed to be trying to think of how she could lie her way out of the question, until suddenly her composure broke and she started to sob.

"I'm sorry Karolina. I didn't want anyone to know what happened. It was so hurtful!" Violet dabbed at her eyes for a few seconds then took a deep breath, before whispering to Karolina, "Robert's message told me to come to his room as soon as Percy was asleep. He knew Percy takes sleeping powders and he told me I would be able to sneak out without waking him. I know I shouldn't have, but I did what he said. He said being in the same hotel was too good a chance to miss!" Again, Violet broke into sobs. "He told me to come to his room but when I knocked at his door, he told me to go away! He got really nasty. Called me . . . some horrible things. Said he didn't want to see me ever again!"

Karolina reached across the table to hold her hand. Whatever the rights or wrongs of what she had done, the poor girl had obviously been terribly hurt. Noticing that Violet had already finished her cocktail, Karolina signalled for Mario to bring another round.

Chapter 19

Alex made his way downstairs and to the room so recently occupied by Robert Smith. Taking the key from his pocket, he opened the door and entered. He stopped just inside the door and scanned the room from that point. The bloodstains on the carpet reminded him of the scene as he had discovered it just two days ago. His mind superimposed Robert Smith's body on top of the bloodstains. What had been a pile of clothes dumped on the floor had been neatly folded and stacked on the bed, presumably by the major or the sergeant when they had searched the room. The papers from the briefcase had also been neatly stacked on the bed. Alex crossed to the bed and flipped through the papers, looking for Robert's evidence against Ronald. In a brown paper file, he found three used envelopes addressed to Ronald. Removing the first letter from its envelope, he quickly confirmed that it was in fact an intimate love letter. After checking the signature, he placed it back in the envelope and looked down at the three letters in his hand, pondering what was the right thing to do. He had only been a naval officer for five years, but he had quickly learnt the lesson that rules were not to be followed blindly. There had been numerous instances where the right or moral thing to do had meant turning a blind eye to the relevant rules and orders. As he said this to himself, he remembered that the very saying, 'turning a blind eye' had originated with England's most famous naval officer, Nelson himself. Suddenly decisive, he slipped the incriminating letters into his inside jacket pocket. Having gone through the remaining papers, nothing else appeared to be of interest. He stood there in front of the bed, with the bedside table and the half-burnt armchair to his right and noticed again the wastepaper basket next to the chair. Something in his brain was trying to make its way from his subconscious into his conscious mind. Inside the wastebasket was some crumpled brown paper and an empty wooden cigar box, that would have held maybe five or ten small cigars. He reached down and pulled out the brown wrapping paper and smoothed it out on the bed. Turning the wrapping paper over he saw 'R. Smith' scrawled in purple lavender ink across it. In his head alarm bells were ringing and he knew that in some way this was significant. As he stared down at his discovery, his head was suddenly wrenched backwards. A strong arm across his throat held him in a headlock. He gripped the arm in both hands and desperately tried to pull it down from his throat. As he struggled, the only thing stopping him from falling backwards was the strength of that choke hold. He attempted to shout for help, but all that emerged was a crude coughing sound. A harsh voice warned him, "Keep on struggling my friend and you'll become better acquainted with this little stinger I have pricking your kidneys."

Alex realised for the first time that there was a sharp pain in his side. The man's other hand must be holding a knife, pressed into his ribs. Alex was now struggling to remain conscious, unable to breathe.

"Now unless you want to end up the same as your friend did, you're going to tell me what you've done with the emeralds!"

The man must have been well practiced in his technique, because now he relaxed the choke hold slightly so that Alex could answer. Alex dragged a deep breath down into his lungs and gasped, "I have no idea what you're talking about."

Instantly the full power of the choke hold was replaced and Alex was unable to breathe again. "Now come along Mr. Armstrong. This is only going to end badly for you, unless you tell me what you and Mr. Smith did with my emeralds."

"YOU THERE!!! STOP THAT THIS INSTANT!!!" A stentorian bellow came from the doorway, causing Alex's attacker to suddenly pivot round to his left. Alex was pulled along with him. Alex shifted, to try to get his legs underneath him again and almost succeeded, but his injured and weaker leg gave way. Suspended by his throat, still in the choke hold, Alex's full weight hung there. His attacker had only two choices, join Alex as he collapsed on the floor, or release the choke hold. He let Alex fall to the floor with a crash.

"You man!! What the hell do you think you're playing at!"

Alex lay gasping for breath on the floor, with his attacker standing over him, knife in hand. Alex recognised him as the guest with red hair. Blocking the door to the hotel room stood an apparition. Dressed in a russet smoking jacket, wing collared white shirt, white bow tie and wearing the most garish Scottish plaid trousers Alex had ever seen, was Lieutenant-Colonel Pinky Pinkersley!

"You stupid fat clown!" snapped Arrowsmith. "Clear off before I prick you with my little knife here!"

Behind the older man's bushy moustache, his face was turning red. "You can try if you want my young fellah me lad, but others better than you have tried and failed. Why when I was in the Ashanti war, the warrior queen . . . "

Murder on Malta

Letting out a strangled scream Arrowsmith leapt forward and slashed across at waist height to open up the older man's stomach. Or he would have done, if the old man had still been stood there. With a lightness belying his weight the colonel took a half a step back, staying just out of Arrowsmith's reach. With his right leg bent and to the front, his left leg nearly straight and behind him, and his left arm raised behind him, the old man raised his walking stick to point directly at Arrowsmith face. "Going to be like that is it me lad. In that case . . . En Garde!"

The very last thing that Arrowsmith expected, was for the old man to move from defence to attack. Keeping his back foot in place, he pushed his right foot forward and stabbed into Arrowsmith's solar plexus with the tip of his walking stick. Arrowsmith let out a gasp of pain and tried to sweep his knife across his attacker's arm, but the old man had already taken a half step back and was watching Arrowsmith's eyes with a look of pleasure behind his bushy white moustache. Angrily Arrowsmith tried a stab at the older man's eyes but the colonel parried it and cracked his stick down on Arrowsmith's forearm. Now overcome with rage, Arrowsmith thrust his knife towards the colonel's throat and charged at the old man. With a delicate flick of the wrist, the colonel's walking stick parried Arrowsmith's arm downwards and to the side and away from him, but Arrowsmith brute force was too much. Arrowsmith crashed into the colonel chest to chest and the knife plunged into the old man's side. Arrowsmith's mad charge knocked the colonel backwards and to the hall floor. Arrowsmith continued his rush and leaped over the old man into the hallway. The commotion had caused other guests to emerge and they stared at Arrowsmith as he stood over the colonel on the floor. He turned and looked back into the bedroom and saw that Alex had risen to his feet. Uttering another shout of rage, he took to his feet and ran down the corridor as fast as he could, until he disappeared down the stairs and out of sight.

Alex's first concern was for Lieutenant-Colonel Pinkersley. Alex knelt over the old man. "Are you hurt sir? Is everything okay?"

"No it damn well isn't! Blighter stuck his blasted knife in my hipflask! That's my Macallan ten-year-old scotch soaking my jacket! Get after him man! Get after him!"

Alex reached for his walking stick from where it lay on the floor and used it to lever himself back to his feet. He looked despairingly down the hallway in the direction that Arrowsmith had escaped. Just as he was about to give up and turn back to the colonel, Karolina came into sight. She looked calm and relaxed, walking casually from around the far corner of the hallway.

"Quickly!" Alex shouted to her, "It was Arrowsmith. He's the murderer! Get after him, but be careful, he has a knife!"

For a split-second Karolina hesitated, then she spun on her heel and sprinted after Arrowsmith. She took the steps down to the lobby two at a time, catching on to the banister on each landing to spin her around the corners. She was grateful that she was wearing her culottes and had her Musette bag over her shoulder. She came off the last few steps into the lobby still sprinting at top speed, then stumbled to a halt. All the heads of the guests had turned at her dramatic arrival. Every conversation had stopped and every eye was on her. Arrowsmith was not to be seen anywhere in the lobby. She stood there for several seconds, considering her options. Should she backtrack and search the floors she had passed on the way down, or the public rooms on the ground floor, or check outside the hotel. At that moment, the concierge entered from the street and through the open door Karolina saw a karozzin passing at a brisk trot going up the hill to the right, with Arrowsmith in the back.

Karolina ran at top speed through the lobby causing some of the guests and the concierge to dive out of her way as she passed. As she came outside into the bright sunlight, she quickly scanned the broad street for another karozzin to use to catch Arrowsmith. To her right there were two karozzins, but neither had a horse in the shafts. The two horses were at the water trough in front of the hotel, with four boys brushing them down. To anyone else viewing the scene, there would have been no option other than to run up the hill, hoping for some divine intervention. Karolina was a girl from Texas. Brought up on a ranch, with cattle and horses in constant proximity. A horse, saddled or not, was just a convenient everyday means of getting from A to B.

Smiling she approached the boy holding the reins of the nearest horse and took the reins from his surprised unresisting fingers. Holding the reins in her left hand against the horse's neck, she swung her right leg up and over the horse's back. The horse stood stock still for a split second, unused to the feeling of a rider on his back, then recovering reared up, front legs high off the cobbled stones. Karolina was an expert horsewoman and not so easily dislodged. Next the horse skittered round to the right, through three hundred and sixty degrees, trying to dislodge its unexpected rider. Karolina calmly waited until the horse was pointing in the desired direction, then with firm messages communicated through her knees and her heels, she spurred the horse forward, up the hill. The

Murder on Malta

horse still tossing its head from side-to-side broke into a the street. From the corner of her eye Karolina caught a the owner of the horse, half risen from his seat in front of the cafe, mouth falling open, at a loss for any appropriate words.

Lying low over the horse's withers, she raced up the street with passersby scattering in surprise. The street rose steeply up the hill then bent sharp right then sharp left. As she reached the brow of the hill, she hoped to see Arrowsmith's *karozzin*, but it was already out of sight. Passing out of the narrow confines of the city she entered a spacious plaza. The only exit was a wide road leading from the plaza down towards the docks, and Arrowsmith's hopes of escape. Karolina galloped from the plaza down the road and into a formal garden interwoven with wide carriageways. Catching sight of a carriage moving away through the gardens she spurred the horse on to follow it. The carriage was only moving at a trot and within seconds she was alongside. She leaned down from the horse and looked back into the rear seat of the *karozzin*. She saw Arrowsmith's surprised face looking back up at her. Swinging round in front of the *karozzin*, she swung down from the horse while it was still in motion. She blocked the path of the *karozzin*, holding her hand up in front of the carriage in the universal sign to halt. She stood her ground as the driver reined his carriage in. In three quick steps Karolina was at the side of the *karozzin*. In those few seconds Arrowsmith had been struggling with something inside his jacket. With a snarl he finally pulled his knife free from his jacket and held it up to face Karolina.

His snarl froze on his lips, as he looked into her steady eyes. She had pulled her Smith and Wesson .38 from her Musette bag. She held it in her right hand, pointed rock steady between his eyes. In a steady calm voice she said, "In Texas we having a saying about someone stupid enough to bring a knife to a gun fight. Want to hear how it ends?"

Chapter 20

Arrowsmith stood in the back of the carriage, looking at Karolina weighing up his options. Would a pretty young thing like Karolina have the guts to shoot him if he ran for it?

As if reading his thought's Karolina, still speaking in a calm measured voice said, "You may be wondering if I have the nerve to kill a man. I have. But that seems to me unnecessarily excessive. To begin with, my first shot would be just to wound you." So saying she slowly lowered her gun that had been aiming directly at his face, to aim at a point about six inches below his belt buckle. "It's up to you of course, but it will be less painful for you if you drop that knife!"

As he paused in thought, deciding if Karolina was really just bluffing, there was a huge bang!

Arrowsmith jumped and a look of complete shock crossed his face, then he slowly looked down towards where Karolina's gun was still aimed.

Gradually realising that he was unhurt, he looked up at Karolina's laughing face. "That was just the naval timing cannon," she said, "Next time it will be my little gun – so drop that knife NOW!"

Finally convinced of the very real danger he was in Arrowsmith hurried to comply. At the same time Karolina became aware of a loud and rapid crashing of boots from behind her. Approaching at a jog, were six soldiers, with Sergeant Moore in the lead. When they reached Karolina, still holding her gun on Arrowsmith, the sergeant drew his own pistol and ordered "Halt". The squad of soldiers crashed to a standstill in unison.

Murder on Malta

"Good morning, ma'am. Hopes as you're enjoying your stay on Malta. We was just on our ways over to the hotel on Major Fleming's orders, to find and happrehend a Mr. Arrowsmith for questioning, when we noticed you and this gentleman having discussions. May I take it ma'am that this here gentleman is the afore said Mr. Arrowsmith?"

"Indeed it is Sergeant Moore and I would greatly appreciate your assistance in escorting the afore said gentleman back to the hotel."

"Looks to me ma'am, that you is doin' my work for me, making me look bad and trying to put me out of me job, ma'am."

"Not at all sergeant. I was just out for an afternoon ride in the park on this nice sunny day, when I saw and recognised Mr. Arrowsmith. Please feel free to take Mr. Arrowsmith off my hands at your convenience."

"Right you are ma'am." Turning to the soldiers behind him, who had been watching their conversation with wide grins on their faces, the sergeant barked, "Wipe those smirks of your faces now! Right! One man either side of the prisoner. Two in front. Two behind. Jump to it! Jump to it! And you sir," pointing to Arrowsmith, "Down from the carriage now." When Arrowsmith didn't comply quickly enough, Sergeant Moore bellowed, "Get down NOW! And don't you be thinking about giving me no trouble."

Arrowsmith complied hurriedly without further delay. Karolina swung her right leg easily over her horse's back, remounting her horse effortlessly and gracefully. The escort party formed up and they all began to return to the hotel.

As the party came down the street into view of the hotel, various spectators were grouped outside, exchanging views on Karolina's recent exit from the hotel. They comprised Alex and James, both Mr. Critchley and William, together with waiters and guests from the hotel. Lady Felshaw and her son were also present, Lady Felshaw with her well-practised look of disapproval on her face. Her son however was looking happy and excited by the recent commotion. The owners of the two karozzin and the boys who took care of the horses formed their own little group in front of the café. All gossip and chatter faded into silence as the procession came into sight, coming down the street.

Karolina led the group, still riding the horse bareback. She was followed by Sergeant Moore, pistol drawn marching behind her. Behind the sergeant, the soldiers surrounded Arrowsmith, hands tied. Behind them followed Arrowsmith's karozzin, for no other reason than the driver was enjoying the attention the procession was receiving.

The party came to an orderly halt in front of Major Fleming and Karolina slid down from her horse, handing the reins, with a brief thank you, to one of the boys. The boy stood there staring up at Karolina in awe with his mouth hanging open.

The only person who didn't appear to have been struck dumb was Alex.

"I see you're doing a good job with the staying out of trouble, Karolina."

Chapter 21

"Sergeant Moore reporting sir! Suspect h'apprehended as ordered. He was a threatening Miss McAllister with this 'ere knife at the time sir." Sergeant Moore held up Arrowsmith's knife by the point for Major Fleming to see. "Not that she seemed to be too worried about it mind you sir."

"Good work sergeant. Very good work indeed." Major Fleming was standing with Alex in front of the hotel. "Be so good as to escort the prisoner round to the police station. Ask for Inspector Johnson. He knows all about the case. Tell him I'll be along in a minute and we can start interviewing the prisoner then." The sergeant acknowledged his orders, saluted and made a smart about turn before bellowing out his orders to his men and marching the prisoner and escorts off up the street. The spectators and hotel guests, recognising that this was the end of the show for today, began to disperse.

"Excuse me major, it might be worth your while to hang around for a few minutes longer. I think we may be able to provide you with some more evidence."

The major looked at Alex quizzically. "Certainly Lieutenant. As I've remarked earlier, I've come to appreciate your observational skills. Show me what you've discovered."

Alex led the group back in to the lobby and across to the reception desk. Mr. Critchley had returned to his post after watching the excitement in front of his hotel. "Mr. Critchley. May I ask you some questions about the night of Mr. Smith's murder?"

"Of course, Lieutenant Armstrong. I will assist in any way I can."

"I understand that he stopped at the reception desk on his way to his room? Can you tell me again what he did?"

"Certainly. He wrote a message for Mrs. Osborne. That is not the sort of behaviour that we expect from our guests. Most reprehensible."

"Quite right too Mr. Critchley. But Miss McAllister also mentioned something about picking up his messages?"

"He did. He had one message in his pigeonhole. Or package to be more precise."

"Wrapped in brown paper, with his name on it?"

"Why yes lieutenant. Exactly as you say. He seemed quite surprised to see it."

"And do you by any chance know who left it for him?"

"I'm sorry lieutenant, it must have been when William was behind the desk. You are aware that it's not my job to work reception. I employee staff for such menial work."

"Quite so, Mr. Critchley. Perfectly understood. One final question if you don't mind. I was in the lobby, when Mr. Smith came down somewhat later in the evening. He spoke to you again and you gave him a sheet of paper. Could you tell me what that was?"

"Quite correct lieutenant. It was the arrivals and departures sheet that is issued by the harbour master, showing the times ships are scheduled to arrive or depart the harbour. Guests refer to it to determine the next ships to leave for their desired location."

"And did Mr. Smith indicate which destination he was interested in?"

"No lieutenant. He appeared to only be interested in what ships would be the first to depart in the morning."

"Thank you, Mr. Critchley. You have been a great help."

Alex turned away from the reception desk and signalled for the major and Karolina to follow as he headed for the stairs to Robert Smith's room. As he climbed the stairs slowly, with the aid of his walking stick, Karolina began to question him.

"How do you think Arrowsmith and Robert knew each other? Was Robert in debt to him due to his gambling?"

"I don't believe so. When Arrowsmith attacked me in Robert's room, he thought I was working with Robert. He demanded I give him 'the emeralds'."

"So maybe Robert had bought emeralds with the money he got from selling the secret codebooks to the Austrians and Arrowsmith found out and decided to steal them?"

"I don't think it was that either."

"So maybe they were working together and Arrowsmith killed him for his share?"

Alex shook his head. "I don't think so."

Karolina was getting frustrated now. "Well maybe Arrowsmith was Robert's long-lost brother and he killed him to inherit a gold mine in Africa! Alex, if you don't hurry up and tell us what you think happened there may be another murder!"

"I'm hoping we'll find some evidence that will tell us not just the motive, but how Arrowsmith and Robert came to blows. If I'm right neither one of them had met the other until Arrowsmith murdered Robert."

By now they had unlocked and entered Robert's room and Alex walked over to the wastepaper basket. Picking up the brown paper, he laid it smoothed out on the bed and placed the empty cigar box on top of it. "See how the creases in the paper match the shape of the cigar box?" he asked. He turned them ov Robert's name on the reverse. "It was addressed to "Mr. R. Smith. That ink is very distinctive. It's from the pen on reception."

"So, you believe this was the package he collected from reception?" asked the major.

"I do. I also believe the box contained the emeralds that Arrowsmith wanted."

The major said thoughtfully "Emeralds are often smuggled from West Africa particularly Nigeria through intermediary ports like Valletta and Gibraltar and then into Europe. The blue green emeralds can be worth more, weight-for-weight, than diamonds," said Major Fleming.

"Emeralds have been highly prised for thousands of years. We even find them in the Pharoh's tombs in Egypt," added Karolina.

"I think Robert came into possession of a considerable fortune unexpectedly and that's why he was planning to leave on the next possible ship. If I'm right, the emeralds that were the cause of Robert's death are still here, in this room. Can I ask us to split up and search? Remember were looking for something small enough to fit inside this cigar box."

Karolina took Robert's briefcase and contents and Major Fleming took his suitcases and clothing. Alex looked in and under the bed. After thirty minutes they had no results to show for their work and they started to look elsewhere in the room. Alex looked at the partly burnt armchair and lifted off the blackened towels that had put the fire out, then lifted out the seat cushion.

"Nothing?" asked Karolina with her fist on her hips.

Murder on Malta

"Nothing," agreed Major Fleming.

Alex straightened up, "Nothing here either, but I'm sure of my theory. The emeralds are here in this room, somewhere!" He looked down at his hands, black and dirty from the half-burnt fabric. In exasperation he went into the bathroom and washed them in the sink. Looking around for a towel he realised that both towels were sitting on the armchair and would be just as filthy. Looking around he saw the cast brass paper roll holder, the casting proudly proclaiming it had been made by 'Sanitary Paper Co., of Bury Street, London, 1884". He pulled out a couple of feet of paper from the roll, to the accompaniment of a noisy rattling from the old, worn-out holder.

"Alex, I think we're going to have to give up, at least for the time being. Maybe Arrowsmith will know where Robert hid the emeralds," called Karolina from the bedroom.

After several seconds of silence Major Fleming asked "Alex, are you OK?"

Alex was still standing in the door to the bathroom, with a slow bemused smile spreading across his face. He threw the tissue paper he had been using to dry his hands into the wastepaper basket and asked Karolina, "Karolina, would you come over here and hold out your hands, together if you please?"

Karolina did as he asked and she and Major Fleming watched Alex in excitement as he turned around.

Grasping the roll of tissue paper in his right hand, he pulled it towards the left and removed it from the holder. Inside the roll of tissue paper was a metal, spring-loaded spindle. It was designed to secure the roll of paper in the holder. Carefully, Alex twisted one end of the metal tube until, with an audible 'twang', the end came away revealing a spring attached to the shorter end. Turning back to Karolina, he slowly tilted the longer end of the tube over her hands until a beautiful stream of blue green emeralds cascaded out of the tube to form a mound in Karolina's hands.

Chapter 22

"Alex, you are absolutely incredible!" exclaimed Karolina.

"I have to second the motion, Lieutenant Armstrong. You've done an amazing job! My congratulations!"

"There is still one more mystery to resolve," said Alex. "How did Robert get hold of these emeralds? I think I have an answer for that too. Can I suggest we put the emeralds back in that cigar box and take them with us downstairs to reception. I think I can put the final piece of the puzzle in place."

Major Fleming dutifully retrieved the cigar box and Karolina reluctantly emptied what she now called 'her emeralds' into it. They then both followed Alex downstairs. Alex led the way to the reception desk which was now manned by William, while Mr. Critchley busied himself with the important task of greeting the guests as they came and went from the hotel.

Alex addressed William, making sure to talk loudly and clearly, while Karolina and Major Fleming listened, "William perhaps you can help me with a couple of things," and when William nodded, he continued, "First, do you remember just after we checked in, you were speaking to someone at the reception desk. He was dressed in a rather dirty white boiler suit, seemed to be perhaps Moroccan, Algerian or similar? I believe he gave you a brown paper package for a guest?"

"I does Lieutenant Armstrong I does. He was in a fearful rush to get back before his ship sailed. He said he had a package that had to get to Mr. Smith. I said I'd give it to him and put it in his pigeonhole. Did I not do the right thing sir?"

Murder on Malta

"No. You absolutely did the right thing. No problem. Now, the second thing you can help me with is a bit of a children's riddle." Dropping his voice to a conversational level, he said "Which gentleman is the taller? Mr. R. Smith, or, Mr. Arrowsmith?"

William looked at Alex puzzled for a few seconds, before replying, "Don't make no sense to me sir. Who is the taller? Mr. R. Smith or Mr. R. Smith? Sorry sir, I just don't get it."

"No William, it's all right. It doesn't make much sense, does it? Well, thank you for helping anyway." Alex turned and moved away with Karolina and the major close behind.

"Alex, that's brilliant! William's deafness meant he couldn't hear the difference between the two names. The guy in the boilersuit wanted to leave the package of emeralds for Mr. Arrowsmith, but William thought he said Mr. R. Smith!"

"Agreed. At that time, Arrowsmith had not yet checked in. William only knew of one guest it could be and that was Mr. R. Smith. He would be horrified if he ever finds out that it was his mistake that led to Robert's death. Later in the evening, when Arrowsmith was checking in, Robert also came down to reception. Arrowsmith heard Robert's name called out by the concierge. He must have realised how easy it was to confuse their two names, and the possibility that his emeralds had been given to the wrong person."

"This has been some exceptional detective work by the two of you," said Major Fleming, "I have to say you have exceeded all my expectations. At the moment I need to get along to the police station and have them formally arrest Arrowsmith, but this evening I would like to show my gratitude by taking the both of you to the nightclub for dinner. Is that okay?"

Murder on Malta

Alex and Karolina were more than happy to accept and agreed to meet the major in the lobby, later that evening.

Chapter 23

That evening, Alex took special care getting dressed for dinner. He really only had his old Royal Navy mess uniform to wear, with the short blue jacket with his rank insignia, but he made sure it looked as clean and smart as it could. He stood in front of the mirror and wondered how the night would go. He suspected the major would be much better dressed, probably wearing an expensive dinner jacket and he'd probably want to dance with Karolina. He knew he was feeling jealous of Major Fleming's smooth easy confidence and the attraction between him and Karolina, but had no idea how to compete, or even if he should try to compete for Karolina's attention. After all, he had come to look on Karolina as a good friend, maybe his closest friend. If she was, then surely, he should do everything he could to make her happy. So why wasn't he encouraging James's friendship with her? He sighed and went to the window to enjoy the view. Dusk was falling and lights were coming on across the harbour and in the moored civilian ships. Alex turned away from the window and left his room. Walking the short distance down the corridor, he knocked on Karolina's door.

After a few seconds, she opened it dressed in a new red silk floor-length evening gown. She was only wearing a minimum of jewellery but looked beautiful. Alex sighed and gave her a ruthful smile. "You look incredible."

"Thank you, sir, a girl always like to hear that," she replied with a small laugh. "This is what I bought when I was out shopping with Maude. Like it?"

"You make it look fantastic," replied Alex. "Shall we go down and see if the gallant major has arrived?"

"Certainly," said Karolina, as she stepped out of her room and locked the door. Moving round to his good side, so that Alex could use his walking stick, she linked her arm through his and they made their way down to the lobby.

Major Fleming was sitting in a chair in the lobby and stood up as soon as he saw them. "Ready to celebrate?" he asked?"

"Absolutely. Lead on James," replied Karolina.

They left the hotel and walked three abreast down the steps and along the street to 'The-Hole-In-The-Wall' nightclub. As before, the doorman recognised the major, but this time, instead of a booth, they were led to a table laid for dinner, with a good view of the dance floor and stage. As soon as Coco saw the group, she came over to take their order for drinks. The major ordered a bottle of champagne for the table. As they sat back and enjoyed the house band, Karolina asked, "Do you think Maria will be singing tonight?"

"I would think so. She's here most nights and usually sings if she's here."

The major lit a cigarette, then placed it in the ashtray in the middle of the table. Rising from his chair, he said, "This is a great song to dance to. Karolina? Would you like to dance?"

"Why thank you, James." Karolina looked up at James standing next to her with his hand held out, confident of her acceptance. "Yes I think that would be fun!"

Taking her hand, he led her out onto the dance floor where, as Alex watched them, they were soon swept away laughing onto the dance floor surrounded by the other dancers.

Murder on Malta

The major's cigarette had long turned to ashes in the ashtray, when the couple returned from the dance floor, laughing and breathless. Alex smiled up at Karolina and made to rise from his chair, but Karolina put her hand on his shoulder and still laughing said, "No. Please don't get up Alex." She dropped down heavily into her seat. "That was fun! But now I'm hungry. Let's order dinner!"

The major signalled to Coco, who brought over their menus and slapped them down hard in front of the major, before turning and stalking away without saying a word. The major shrugged and passed out the menus to Alex and Karolina. All three were hungry by now and wasted no time in decided what to have. The major signalled for Coco again and they placed their orders, the major adding another bottle of champagne to his order. The food when it came was wonderful and while they ate, the major entertained Karolina with endless stories and good conversation. Once the dessert courses were cleared away, Alex excused himself and went to the bar for cigarettes. Major Fleming leant across to Karolina and said, "I really am very grateful for your efforts in solving Robert Smith's murder. I would love to repay you by showing you around the sights of Valletta and the rest of Malta. You missed out on the trip to the Temple of Ggantija. I could take a few days off and take you to Gozo as well if you wished?"

"Thank you, James. It is somewhere I intend to see. But don't you think maybe Alex would like to come with us too?"

The major sat back and looked at Alex standing at the bar. "I suppose he might, but don't you think it might be a lot for him, physically? It might be better for him to take it easy at the hotel."

Murder on Malta

When Alex returned from the bar, James addressed them both, "You know what, you and Alex really did a magnificent job finding Robert Smith's murderer."

"As I said when we started," Karolina paused as she turned and smiled at Alex, "we make a great team. He's the eyes and I'm the brain!"

"Now if you could only turn your analytical and observational skills to our other mystery and find out who is conducting the espionage, I would shower you both with gifts beyond your wildest dreams."

"Be careful James," laughed Karolina, I have some pretty wild dreams!"

"I would be very, very, careful, major," said Alex quietly, "The answer may not be that far away at all."

Major Fleming instantly seemed to sober up and become serious. "When you say something like that Lieutenant, I've come to realise it's wise to shut up and listen. You have my complete attention."

"Likewise, Alex" said Karolina, leaning in more closely, "What has Sherlock Holmes come up with now?"

"Major, have you noticed that quite luxurious steam yacht, currently moored in the harbour, in front of the hotel?"

"I know the ship you are referring to Lieutenant."

"The ship is right in front of the window in my room. As I was watching the ship, they began unloading some red empty ten-gallon drums. They used a hoist and crane to load them into a small boat alongside. I assumed that the drums had contained petrol for their auxiliary electricity generator. They used the hoist to lower the drums, one at a time into the small boat."

Murder on Malta

"Okay, I get the picture. Why is that important?" said James.

"I see what Alex means, James," said Karolina excitedly. "If I was doing that job, I'd have just tossed the empty drums down to be caught by one of the men in the boat. Even if they were dropped in the sea, so what? They'd float."

"Exactly. So the only explanation I could think of was that they weren't empty, but contained something heavy that they didn't want to lose overboard."

"So, you think we have the ship that's been bringing in leaflets and posters hidden inside petrol drums? And probably the one that's sending the coded radio messages. This is great Alex, but we still don't know who the agent 'Sparrow' is or where they're based!" said the major.

"Have patience major," said Karolina with a half-hidden smile on her face. "I know that look in Alex's eyes. He's enjoying himself and there's more to come!"

Alex smiled back at her. "Every time I've looked at it, it's been dressed overall as we say in the navy. That means it's strung with flags from stem to stern. The flags are what we call signal flags. Individual signal flags that can either represent a frequently used word, like 'harbour', 'cargo', etc, or they can represent letters in the alphabet. When I first noticed the ship, the flags happened to be spelling out a message about unloading a cargo, probably just a random chance I thought. Yesterday, they were in a different sequence, acknowledging receipt of a message." Alex had the complete attention of the others now.

"Isn't that a pretty stupid way to send a secret message?" asked Karolina. "It's wide out in the open!"

Murder on Malta

James answered her, "Believe me there have been plenty of examples where simpler methods have been used. During the war, the Russians would send orders and battle plans in plain text – not in code, perhaps believing that no one would be listening to their radio traffic. That ended in disaster for them, but in other circumstances simple methods have proved very effective. Our spies obviously didn't expect to come up against Lieutenant Armstrong's observational skills, or it maybe it's that they are simply arrogant."

Alex continued, "Looking down from the hotel, we have a good view of the long roof terrace on top of the 'Hole-In-The-Wall' club. Have you ever noticed how Maria spends so much time arranging and rearranging the flower pots along the edge of the terrace? They've been in different sequences every day. Different sequences of blue and yellow flower pots." Alex paused to take a sip from his champagne coupe. "You know that when I was serving at sea, I was a signals lieutenant? A signals lieutenant almost lives and breathes Morse code. I started wondering what if the blues and yellows were dots and dashes? And that was the other half of the conversation. The date and time to bring 'the cargo' to the nightclub. I got the confirmation, if you still need it, when I went to the bar for cigarettes just now, they had left the door to the corridor behind the bar open. Stacked in the corridor are the usual crates of beer, cases of wine and so on, but also a red 10-gallon petrol drum. It had been modified so that the whole end of the drum was a lid and the lid was lying next to it on the floor."

Karolina nodded. "You know I never did like the way that Maria simpered over you, Alex. She was obviously a spy trying to pump you for information."

"I thought she was just being very nice. Some women do find me quite attractive you know."

"Oh no. You're not that attractive. She definitely wanted secret information."

Alex looked a little disappointed until he saw that Karolina was trying to hold back laughter. Trying to pretend he hadn't taken her seriously he continued, "When we had decoded the reports and discovered the agent's code name was 'Sparrow', Ronald told us all quite a lot about the life of sparrows. Turns out he is quite the amateur ornithologist. What I didn't know until Ronald told us is that the sparrow is the national bird of Italy. However, one thing I did know already, from being brought up in an old manor house and farm, is that sparrows love to nest in holes in the old stone walls. And here we are, in 'The Hole-In-The-Wall' club.

Major Fleming said nothing. He looked across the dance floor to the stage, to where Maria was singing with the band. After several minutes, still without taking his eyes off Maria, he spoke quietly to Alex and Karolina. "If you are correct and I have no doubt that you are, then I need to set up some discreet observation to see who comes and goes over the next few days. The next time the steamship comes into harbour, we'll catch them smuggling red-handed. Then we will bring in anyone suspicious who was been visiting the club. With that many in custody, one or more are sure to spill the beans and give evidence against the rest. So, if you'll excuse me, I need to get a surveillance operation up and running as soon as possible. If you don't mind, I'll leave you both to enjoy the music. Eat and drink as much as you want, I'll tell Coco to charge it to me." Standing, he shook Alex's hand and bent down kissed Karolina on her cheek, before leaving the club.

After James had left, they sat in silence for a while until Karolina turned to Alex and said, "Alex, if I asked you to trust me, would you do something for me, even if you didn't want to?"

Alex wasn't sure what Karolina planned but instinctively he trusted her, so he nodded.

She rose from her chair and came to stand on Alex's left side. She slipped her right arm underneath Alex's left arm and lifted. Reluctantly Alex rose to his feet. She Interleaved her finger with his and taking some of his weight, slowly took a small step away from the table. Alex felt embarrassed at this close physical contact and worriedly looked round believing that people would be looking at him, unable to walk by himself without help from this beautiful young girl. Anger started to rise in him and he was at the point of refusing to move and insisting on sitting down again, when Karolina said softly, "Just trust me."

She took another small step towards the dance floor and Alex went with her, carefully maintaining his balance. They reached the dance floor in small slow steps and without Karolina losing her grip on his arm. As they stood at the edge of the dance floor, Karolina moved round in front of him and positioned his right arm around to her back, still holding his left hand tightly in her right. Moving in close to his body she said, "I think we can do this, don't you? So long as we do it together," She laid her head on Alex's shoulder and she and Alex began to sway to a slow romantic waltz.

Chapter 24

It was two days later that Karolina and Alex left Valletta to journey to the northern island of Gozo. With the excitement of catching Robert Smith's killer, then discovery of the spy ring, Karolina had almost forgotten that her whole purpose of coming to Malta was to visit the temple of Ggantija on Gozo. After all it was the oldest human structure in the world. As an archaeologist she was excited to see it, but she had been surprised that Alex also wanted to see it. In truth, Alex had not been that excited, but when she had suggested it to him, he had readily agreed. If he was honest with himself, he was grateful for any excuse to postpone a decision on his future.

Major Fleming had come to the hotel to see them off. He was disappointed that his ongoing surveillance of the night club meant he couldn't accompany Karolina, but had arranged for a car to take them to the northern tip of Malta, where they could catch a ferry to Gozo, and had personally recommended a hotel to them for their stay on Gozo.

Early this morning Karolina and Alex had caught a small ferry boat across the harbour from Valletta to Sliema and were now anxiously waiting for their driver to make himself known.

"This must be him," said Karolina as a short round-faced man in traditional baggy trousers, loose white shirt and a flat cap came along the sea wall towards them.

"Lady Karolina," he called, "Lieutenant Armstong sir. My name is Andrew de Bono. I am to take you to Marfa for the ferry to Gozo, yes?"

Murder on Malta

"Yes indeed," replied Karolina enthusiastically, as the driver picked up their four pieces of luggage and led them to his vehicle. "We're going to Gozo to see the Temple of Ggantija!"

"Indeed my lady. That is a wonderous temple. You know perhaps that it was built by a female giant called Sunsuna who lived on Gozo? It is said she married a Maltese farmer and had a baby boy."

"Really? How big was she?"

"I'm sorry my lady I do not know, but she must have been very large and very strong. It is said she carried the stones to build the temple on her head as she carried her baby in her arms. And the stones are very, very big! But our women are also very, very strong!" he finished with a laugh and began to strap the larger two suitcases to the rear of his car. It was a small pre-war Fiat, painted bright blue, with a white canvas roof. The wooden spokes of its wheels added to its festive appearance being painted bright red. Alex opened the small rear door and offered his hand to Karolina as she mounted the running board and took her seat. Alex placed his good foot onto the running board and heaved himself in next to her. After cranking the engine into life, Andrew slid into the front seat behind the steering wheel and with a crash of gears pulled away.

Sliema was much smaller than Valletta and the terraces of businesses, stores and houses soon gave way to individual buildings as the car climbed steadily out of the town. They took the coast road North, with the Mediterranean Sea on their right. As they left the town of Sliema the road became a gravel track and climbed up over high hills or ridges before sweeping down into small rocky bays along the coast. Several of the rocky headlands they passed had tall square defensive towers on them. As they passed close to

Murder on Malta

one particular tower Karolina leant forward and asked the driver, "Were those towers built by the Knights of Malta?"

"Yes Lady. The Knights of the Hospital of St. John built them to defend Malta. All Europe knows of the great siege of 1565 when 50,000 Ottomans were defeated by 500 Knights of Malta and just 2,000 soldiers! The Ottoman fleet of hundreds of ships besieged Valletta for half a year, but we never gave in! If we had then Suleiman the Terrible would have taken Malta and then surely Sicily and on to Italy! We threw the Ottomans back into the sea and killed half of their army. We Maltese stopped the Ottomans and saved Europe!"

"Wow!" said Karolina, "You must be a very well-educated man Andrew to know so much history."

Andrew turned to smile back at her before saying, "Yes my lady. Andrew de Bono is a well-educated man, I have read many books it is true, but even our children know the story of the great siege. All children know this because we have a great holiday every September 8th to celebrate our victory, and our children love the feast and the carnival."

Karolina smiled back at him as he turned back to the watch the road. She wondered what the festival must be like and hoped she might return to Malta to see it. Relaxing in the back of the small car she turned her attention back to the landscape. The greater part of the countryside seemed to be barren rocky hillsides broken up by patches of small terraced fields. Hedges and fences were absent and instead fields and terraces were separated by low dry-stone walls. Many of the walls were decorated by sporadic clumps of prickly pear cactus, some ten or twelve feet tall. They had passed several small hamlets with just a handful of cottages situated within feet of the road. As they passed through yet another, Alex noticed an elderly woman, dressed head to toe in black, sprinkling a white powder in front of her doorway.

"Andrew, was she sprinkling salt in front of her doorway? Is that to keep out bugs?"

"Salt, yes sir, but not to keep out bugs. Country folk believe it is bad luck to sweep out their cottages when it is dark. They sweep out the dust into the road only in daylight and then they must sprinkle a line of salt across their doorstep to stop bad luck and the devil from entering!"

Karolina and Alex looked back at the old lady and both wondered about what her life was like in this remote and rocky land, but their car soon swept them away around another bend in the winding gravel road and the old lady disappeared from their sight.

They had now covered ten or twelve miles, and the car crested one more of the many hills but this time the bay revealed in front of them was the largest yet. Out in the middle of the bay rose a low rocky island, deserted except for a gleaming white statue at its highest point.

"Andrew, what is that statue on that island?" asked Alex.

"That is the island of St. Paul sir, and this is the bay of St. Paul and the statue is of St. Paul himself. You must surely already know of the story of St. Paul." Alex nodded knowledgably, but Karolina looked at him out of the corner of her eye, and couldn't hide her laughter.

Alex looked a little affronted, but said, "Yes, of course Andrew, but perhaps you could refresh Miss McAllister's memory for us?"

Andrew continued happily. "St. Paul was shipwrecked here, on that very island many, many years ago when the Romans ruled Malta. It was a very big miracle that he and the hundreds of others on the ship all swam ashore and no one died. But we Maltese are very friendly, very nice people, so we showed those who had swam ashore great kindness and built a fire to warm them. When St. Paul reached for some firewood, a very poisonous viper bit him in his hand. He should have died, but we saw it was a miracle that he survived and that truly he was a saint. To thank the people of Malta, St. Paul he made the poison in all our snakes and scorpions disappear. No more poisonous snakes on Malta! We saw it was another very great miracle and our island became the first Christian island in the world!"

While he had been talking Karolina had been looking at the buildings in the village of St. Paul, as they passed through. "Alex, look," she said, pointing at a baroque styled church as they passed it. "What time is it? That church has two clock towers, but each clock has a different time. One must be broken."

"No, not broken my lady. Many of our churches have two towers and two clocks, but always one clock is made wrong on purpose."

"Why on earth do you do that?" asked Karolina

Andrew turned to look at her with a smile on his face and laughed. "It is to confuse the Devil my lady!"

Karolina looked at Alex with a puzzled expression on her face, but all Alex could do was shrug his shoulders with a look on his face that said "don't ask me!"

"Seems to be doing a good job of confusing us too!" said Karolina.

Murder on Malta

The car rattled and bounced on over the gravel track, climbing up from St. Paul's Bay into the hills, away from the coast. Five or six miles later the track came out onto the top of a ridge of hills, with the road sweeping away before them, down from the hills to another bay.

"This is Melieha Bay," called out Andrew. See the very beautiful church on the hill here? It is very old. Inside is a cave, where it is said the goddess Calypso was worshipped before St. Paul made it into a Christian church."

"Calypso is the one that kept Odysseus prisoner for seven years?" asked Karolina.

"Yes my lady. You know our history very well," replied Andrew. "Perhaps when you are on Gozo you will see her home where she kept Odysseus prisoner in her cave. We are not far from the ferry to Gozo now my lady. Just another mile or so."

It seemed that Andrew was familiar with the concept of a country mile, since it seemed like at least three or four miles, after the track had zig-zagged down to Melieha bay, that they finally arrived in the small harbour of Marfa, on the northern tip of Malta. Alex and Karolina climbed down from the little Fiat stiff and bruised from the bumpy ride while Andrew unloaded their luggage and walked with them to the small white steamboat tied up at the short jetty. After being paid, including a generous tip and thanks for all his stories from Karolina, Andrew shook hands with Alex and left the pair at the gangway onto the boat. A sailor from the boat picked up their luggage and followed them on board, finding them a wooden slatted bench seat in the sun on the forward deck.

Karolina said, "I didn't expect the boat to be a paddle steamer. I've never been on one before. I've only heard of them on the Mississippi river."

"Those would have been sternwheelers. This is a sidewheeler. There are still quite a few of those about. On the Isle of Wight where I grew up, they're still in regular use as ferries."

"Do you think you'll be going back to the Isle of Wight after Malta?" asked Karolina. She knew Alex was still trying to make up his mind whether to go back to his family farm run by his older brother, or re-enlist with Royal Navy and continue to work as a codebreaker. Either way her time with Alex was coming to an end and she wasn't sure how she felt about that.

"Don't know." Said Alex brusquely. He didn't like being reminded that he still hadn't made a decision. He didn't know why it was so difficult for him to decide. Normally he thought of himself as fairly decisive. This dithering wasn't like him.

The pair fell into an awkward silence as they waited for the paddle steamer to depart.

Just five minutes later, the crew made themselves busy with the mooring ropes, and then the great paddlewheels at the side of the boat began to slowly turn. Soon enough they were thrashing the water vigorously and the boat began to make the crossing to Gozo. The channel between Malta and Gozo was about three miles across, but halfway there the ferry passed close to the much smaller island of Comino. The small island was surrounded by crystal clear and strikingly blue waters with rock arches and caves visible along its rugged coastline. The effect under the cloudless blue sky held them spellbound during the crossing. It seemed like

Murder on Malta

only a few minutes elapsed before the paddle steamer was slowly negotiating its entrance into Mgarr harbour on Gozo. The small harbour was filled with many traditional Maltese fishing boats, each boat a colourful combination of red, blue and yellow. The mirror calm waters of the harbour made the scene even more colourful, reflecting the multiple colours of the boats. Most of the boats were also protected by having the eye of Osiris painted on their bows, a holdover from the days of the Phoenicians.

Rising up on the steep hillsides surrounding the bay stood houses, taverns and shops, but above them, on the hill top to the left stood an ancient defensive fort. Higher still, behind the harbour, stood a tremendous gothic church with multiple spires and an elegant tall steeple reaching up into the sky.

Karolina and Alex quickly disembarked, and immediately secured the services of one of the waiting karozzin, where the driver had chosen to adorn his horse's bridle with several colourful peacock feathers. Karolina had real sympathy for the harnessed horse as it slowly and laboriously pulled the laden carriage up the steep hill, passing close to the beautiful church they had seen from the paddle steamer. Quickly they left the buildings of the town behind and the horse began to pick up speed on the less steep slopes of the gravel cart track leading further inland. As they travelled, Karolina and Alex saw many steep sided hills rising above the countryside, most with small villages and churches on their summits. Many of the churches had twin bell or clock towers. Karolina noticed they had passed several groves of citrus trees that seemed to be surrounded by tall stands of bamboo. When they passed the third such plantation, Karolina leaned forward and asked the driver what was the purpose of the bamboo. The driver leaned back, and said with a smile. "Miss has never seen a storm here on Gozo. The weather is warm but the Mediterranean can send us very bad storms. The bamboo is a windbreak to protect the farmer's orange and lemon trees."

As they crossed the island the beauty and peacefulness seemed to make conversation unnecessary. Eventually the road took a turn and began to make its way back to the coast and they knew they must be nearing their hotel. Suddenly, as they rounded a headland, their destination was laid out in front of them.

Next to them on the top of the headland stood one of the Knights of St. John defensive forts, square and uncompromising. Beneath them, limestone cliffs dropped near vertically to Xlendi bay. The inlet ran deep inland between the sheer cliffs, ending in a sandy beach that crossed from one side of the bay to the other. Behind the sandy beach ran a low sea wall. On the seaward side of the sea wall a line of trees shaded the promenade. On the land side of the sea wall ran a line of a dozen or so low buildings consisting mostly of fishermens' boat houses, small stores but in the centre was the small St. Patrick Hotel. It looked big enough to have only a half a dozen bedrooms, with a small restaurant looking over the sea wall, out to sea.

At this time of day, the sun was shining almost directly into the bay between the white limestone cliffs and turning the crystal-clear waters into a shimmering, glittering dappled blue and turquoise mirror.

The driver pulled the carriage to a halt at the side of the road, looking down on the bay. Without saying a word, he sat and smiled at his two passengers as they took in the view.

After several minutes he said "You happy?"

Karolina was the first to answer. "It's absolutely stunning!"

"I agree. I can't imagine a more beautiful site." said Alex.

"Good," said the driver and nodded happily. Giving a loud click with his mouth urged the horse back into motion. "I take you now to your hotel."

Epilogue

Karolina looked over to her left at Alex sleeping next to her.

A lot had happened in the ten days since she and Alex had danced in the nightclub.

She reached over quietly so as not to disturb him and placed her book on the sand between them. They were spending the day relaxing on the beach in front of the St. Patrick Hotel. Alex and Karolina were leaning back against the hull of a small upturned fishing boat on the clean white sands. They had been watching the fishermen working on their boats out in the bay. The fishermen had been taking palm fronds out in their boats and placing them carefully in the water. Their new friend Joseph, one of those fishermen, had explained that the palm fronds created refuges or shelters the fishermen called 'kannizzati' that attracted dolphin fish or 'lampuki'.

Alex had surprised her by going out with Joseph on his boat several times.

He'd also accompanied her to the temple of Ggantija on several days. She had been so excited to finally see it, walking in amongst the ruins and touch the stones. Even Alex had been suitably impressed by the site. He was used to the megaliths of Stonehenge and had been expecting to see something similar. The much older Temple of Ggantija had surprised him therefore with the intact high stone walls and clearly defined rooms. Seeing the size of the rocks used to create the walls he couldn't believe that it had been

Murder on Malta

achieved by stone-age man and it almost made him believe in the myth of the giantess.

Karolina was convinced he was more confident and less conscious of his injured leg now. One day she had gone shopping in the main town of Victoria and had bought him a swimming costume. When she got back, she'd put it in his hands and told him to get changed. They were going swimming. He'd refused, made excuses and tried to change the subject but she'd just ignored him and got changed herself. When she came back, she was in her modern swimsuit, form-fitting and flattering, with a v-neck and ending mid-thigh. He'd still been standing where she'd left him, looking worried and uncertain. She'd put her fists on her hips and just stared at him, ignoring his protests, until he'd reluctantly given in and still grumbling, left to get changed. When he came back, she'd deliberately made a point of studying his injured leg. It was quite bad, with a loss of muscle and two long jagged scars, one either side of the tibia, still showing the marks of the surgeon's stiches. After looking closely at them she'd declared them 'Not too bad' then pointedly ignored them, and instead teased him about how white his skin was. Together they'd walked out into the bay into the calm, warm Mediterranean until they'd both dived into it. The very salty waters had buoyed them up, and when Alex had surfaced, he had been laughing joyously. Since then, he had swum every day. Lying with her eyes closed a smile spread across her face as she remembered that day.

She didn't realise that Alex had woken up until his voice broke into her thoughts, "It worries me when I see you smiling like that. Makes me wonder who's going to suffer! It's usually me!"

Murder on Malta

"It's your own fault for being so easy to tease. Anyway, why do you assume I'm thinking about you? That's a little conceited, isn't it?" Hastily she tried to think of another subject she might have been considering. "Actually, I was thinking about Major Fleming." She opened one eye and looked sideways at him. Seeing Alex's face fall she decided not to tease him anymore. "The letter he sent you was very complementary about both of us, wasn't it?"

"I'm sure he's feeling very pleased with himself as well. Arrested a murderer and cleaned up a spy ring in the space of a few days."

"Do you think Maria will be convicted of spying?"

"Not sure. Sounded like her underlings are gabbling away non-stop, but I expect the diplomats will get involved and she'll be deported back to Italy. Even if she is, James said he found a lot of papers on their boat that told him a lot about their larger operations. He may get a promotion out of all this."

They both fell silent for a few minutes, thinking about their adventure in Valletta, and enjoying the feeling of the warm sun on their bodies.

"Would you like to go in for another swim?" he asked.

"My but you're keen aren't you?"

"Well it's been years since I last swam. I'd forgotten just how good it felt to swim in the sea!"

Karolina was pleased that Alex enjoyed swimming so much. She was convinced that swimming in the warm supportive Mediterranean waters had had a healing effect on Alex, if not physically, then psychologically. She liked the new confidence he was finding in himself.

Murder on Malta

"Have you thought anymore about what you'd like to do next?" asked Karolina

"I just said, I'd love another swim," answered Alex with a grin on his face.

"Idiot! You know what I mean. What we were talking about earlier. What do you want to do when you get back to England? Sign on again as a codebreaker, or live with your older brother?""

"I knew what you meant. And I have been thinking about it. I still don't know what I want to do, but I've decided what I don't want to do is return to England. Not just yet at any rate." Alex's voice dropped and became more serious. "After four years of war, it feels like the sun has come out after days of cold and rain. I want to see and do things and go places and enjoy myself. Is that very selfish?"

Karolina shook her head. She knew exactly how Alex felt. She had discovered that she had so much more freedom than she had once thought. There was so much that she now realised she could do, that she had never imagined before this journey. So much to see and do that would be both exciting and enjoyable.

"You know, I think I'd like to visit Rhodes," said Karolina thoughtfully. "Or maybe Cyprus. Or Corfu. No, no. What about Alexandria! Or the Pyramids of Egypt, or Luxor! Yes, that's it! We could go and see the Egyptian temples in Luxor! We could visit them all, and more! What do you think Alex?"

Alex felt a thrill go through him at her use of the word 'we'.

Just then a small voice interrupted them.

"Mr. Alex? I'm sorry sir but my father said I should bring this too you straight away!" It was Pietru, the young son of Joseph, the owner of the St. Patrick Hotel.

Murder on Malta

"Not a problem, Pietru. What is it?"

"It's a telegram sir! It came just a minute ago. The post man came here as quickly as he could. He's having a glass of wine now with Papa and I ran here to find you."

Pietru obviously found the arrival of a telegram to be a rare and remarkable event and felt important and excited by his role as messenger. Alex took the small, official looking envelope from the boy's hand, and opened it. Karolina shifted across and leaned on his shoulder so she too could read the message. It was addressed to Alex. "It's from my younger brother Peter," he said as he read it.

URGENT STOP   NEED YOUR SPECIAL DETECTIVE SKILLS STOP   SUSPECT MURDER STOP   COME AT ONCE STOP IF STILL WITH KAROLINA BRING HER TOO STOP   PETER ARMSTONG CHATEAU MARTIGUES COTE D'AZUR   STOP

Murder on Malta

Notes about this book

And now for 'Notes at the end of the book' which both my wife and daughter say is the best part of the book (!). I can sort of understand that. For me researching the history often throws up great stories I would otherwise never have come across.

Firstly, why Malta?

The book is set in Malta for three reasons. Firstly, it's difficult to think of another island that has so much interesting history. Starting with the Temples of Ggantija which are an incredible testimony to the people who lived on Malta and Gozo more than 5,000 years ago. They are claimed to be the oldest free-standing structures on earth. Significantly older than Stonehenge and even the pyramids. Since one of my passions is archaeology, how could I pass up an opportunity to include them in a book? Malta's more 'modern' history isn't any less interesting. In 1530 Charles V, Holy Roman Emperor and king of Spain and Sicily, gave the islands of Malta to the Order of Knights of the Hospital of St John of Jerusalem. Until then, Malta had been part of Sicily (which later became the justification to include it in the 'Italia Irredenta' movement). In the 16th century the Ottoman empire was expanding and attempted to take the island. The result was the 'Great Siege' of 1565, when an invading army of forty thousand Ottomans attempted to take the island from the knights. It was successfully defeated by about five hundred knights of St. John together with five thousand soldiers and civilians. They were led by Grand Master Jean de la Valette who gave his name to Valletta. Another expanding empire set its sights

Murder on Malta

on Malta in 1798, but this time with more success. Napolean invaded Malta and ended nearly three hundred years of rule by the Knights of Malta. The French did not enjoy Malta for long. The inhabitants rebelled and asked Britain for help evicting the French. The British obliged in 1800. Malta then voluntarily became a British protectorate. During the first world war, Malta earned the title of Nurse of the Mediterranean for tending to and nursing more than 100,000 war casualties; truly in the spirit of the Knights Hospitaller. After the first world war, uprisings and demands for independence were endemic throughout the Mediterranean, including on Malta. In 1921, soon after this story is set, the British granted Malta self-governance, although it still remained a British protectorate until 1964. In Italy, following the first world war, Mussolini rose to popularity with the fascist party, promoting the Italia Irredenta movement and Italy's territorial claims on Nice, Malta, Corsica, Savoy, Corfu, Ticino and Dalmatia.

    The second reason to set the story in Malta is more personal. My father, serving in submarines in World War Two, was part of the operation to support the Maltese during the two-and-a-half-year siege by the Germans and Italians. Malta was the recipient of some of the heaviest and most prolonged bombing of WW2, but still it held out. Their attacker's intent was to destroy the Maltese resistance or blockade them to the point of starvation, which they very nearly succeeded in doing. My father told the story of arriving in Valletta when the Maltese were starving, with the submarine stacked to capacity with supplies. Sacks of potatoes were piled high in the gangways making it almost impossible operate the boat! It was another 'Great Siege' but eventually it too was broken. In

Murder on Malta

recognition of the bravery shown by the Maltese population, the island was awarded Britian's highest medal for courage by civilians, the George Cross.

After World War Two my father's submarine was deliberately sunk off St. Paul's Bay, Malta, to act as a sonar training target. Nowadays it's a recreational dive site for experienced divers. It seems somehow appropriate that it has now returned to Malta.

My third reason to set a story on Malta is that, despite the history of fighting and sieges, Malta and Gozo are truly beautiful islands, with a temperate Mediterranean climate, fantastic scenery and beaches and a truly incredible place to visit. If you do, I'm sure you'll enjoy the hustle and bustle of Valletta and the views across the Grand Harbour. Unfortunately, the Grand Harbour British Hotel in the story is fictional, but if it were real, it would occupy the space where the real-life British Hotel and the Grand Harbour Hotel are located.

I would have loved to introduce you to the illustrious 'Alpineer' Lucy Walker, who in real-life was the first woman to climb the Eiger (1864) and the Matterhorn (1871) but unfortunately, she passed away in 1916, so instead the story includes her fictional companion Lily Buchanan, who had similar exploits. Researching the clothing available to female mountain climbers at the time revealed that Burberry, founded in 1856, patented gabardine in 1888. They used pictures of women climbers wearing Burberry climbing suits in their advertising. Their clothing was also used for other adventurous activities such as polar exploration and early flight.

The first documentary evidence of the saying *'bringing a knife to a gunfight'* is attributed to Sean Connery in the movie *'The*

Untouchables' but I personally choose to believe that there is every chance that it may have been an older Texas adage, and to be quite honest it seemed so appropriate that I couldn't resist including it in Arrowsmith's final scene.

It's common knowledge that Britain was heavily bombed during World War Two, but I found that many people don't realise, as Horace comments, that British civilians were both shelled and bombed during World War One. Shelled by the German fleet, and bombed by Gotha bombers and Zeppelins.

Attitudes to security and encoding secret communications in WW1 were very different than today, and some much simpler methods were used. Russia did send crucial battle plans over the radio waves in plain text, allegedly because they thought that no one would be listening at night (unfortunately for the Russians the Germans were). Even the German spy Carl Hans Lody routinely sent telegrams in plain English using the public network. Britain's very effective secret cryptology section was called 'Room 40', and, as told in the story, they had a small office in Brindisi. Alex demonstrated how observant he was when he spotted that Major Fleming of the army's British Military Foot Police used a navy salute rather than the correct army salute. Royal Navy sailors salute with the palm facing down, hidden from sight. The tradition is that sailors worked with tarred ropes and therefore their palms were indelibly stained and 'dirty', and needed to be hidden from view.

Of course, the delightful Lieutenant-Colonel 'Pinky' Pinkersley's is entirely fictious, but the Zanzibar War really was the shortest recorded, lasting approximately 40 minutes, barely time for a '*snifter*'.

Finally, part of the fun in writing a book set just after the first world war is avoiding anachronisms. For example, was it okay to use the term 'boyfriend', and would Major Fleming have used fingerprinting? Well, 'boyfriend' first came into use in 1909, and fingerprints were used in the USA and UK in 1902, although both Mark Twain and Sir Arthur Conan Doyle used them in novels well before that. However, the technology didn't reach Malta until the 1930s. The FBI was originally called the American Bureau of Investigation until its name was changed to the Federal Bureau of Investigation in 1935.

I hope you have enjoyed this book. If you did, then please watch out for the next adventure with Karolina and Alex, book 3, 'Murder on the Cote d'Azur!'

Printed in Great Britain
by Amazon